DAWN LEE MCKENNA'S

WHAT WASHES UP

A *FORGOTTEN COAST* SUSPENSE NOVEL: BOOK THREE

A SWEET TEA PRESS PUBLICATION

First published in the United States by Sweet Tea Press

©2015 Dawn Lee McKenna. All rights reserved.

Edited by Tammi Labrecque

larksandkatydids.com

Cover by Shayne Rutherford

darkmoongraphics.com

Interior Design by Colleen Sheehan

wdrbookdesign.com

For Kat,
Who may one day open this book

CHAPTER
ONE

I t was a windy night out on the bay, very windy for a late-July night without any tropical storms in the area.

Maggie Redmond's long, dark brown hair kept trying to fly out of its clip, and she struggled to get it all tucked and out of her way one-handed. Her right arm, the one she really had a close relationship with, was still in a sling, after she'd been shot by some low-life on her own property.

She gave up on the clip and grabbed onto the portside rail, then looked up at Wyatt Hamilton, who was towering over her, holding binoculars to his face as he looked out to the bay.

She, Wyatt, and Dwight, one of the deputies who worked with them at the Sheriff's office, had taken her Dad's fishing boat out past St. George Island to do a little sunset fishing. Wyatt had just been reeling in a nice-sized redfish when they got the call.

It probably wasn't especially appropriate for them to respond, given that Dwight had had a few beers, Maggie was on leave and one-armed, and Wyatt didn't look especially official in his cargo shorts and red Hawaiian shirt. However, they were already halfway to the location, and would beat the Coast Guard by at least five minutes.

"Can you make anything out yet?" she yelled over the Chris Craft's engine.

"Not really," Wyatt barked. "It's too dark. But they're right, it is on fire."

Michael Vinton and Richard Farrell, two shrimpers that Maggie knew only passingly, had come upon it as they were headed out for the night's work. They'd called the Coast Guard and the Sheriff's Office, and someone at the office had called Wyatt.

Dwight was with them, so it wasn't technically their second date, but Wyatt was a little put out nonetheless.

"Let me look," Maggie yelled up at him. She was short to begin with, but being one-armed besides made her feel even smaller next to Wyatt, who, at six-four, was more than a foot taller than she was.

"No," Wyatt said. "You have one hand and Dwight's hitting every damn wave like he was getting points for it. You'll drop my binoculars."

"No, I won't. Let me look."

"I said 'no,'" Wyatt told her.

He took the binoculars down, looked at her, and gave her an eyebrow waggle. "My mom got me these."

Maggie and Wyatt had worked together at the Sheriff's Office for six years and had become good friends over time. They'd only started seeing each other over the last several weeks. It was, of course, forbidden by the department, so they'd been keeping it quiet. This was fairly easy thus far, as most people thought they acted like an old married couple anyway.

Wyatt had lost his wife to cancer shortly before moving to Apalachicola, and Maggie's friendship had helped him heal. Maggie had lost her ex-husband, who was also her best friend, just a few short weeks ago. Wyatt was helping her heal, too.

Nevertheless, she thought he was a jerk.

As they got closer to their destination, Maggie could see Michael and Richard in the lights of their trawler, anchored just yards away.

A few minutes later, Dwight cut the engine, and they coasted up to about ten yards from the flames. The shrimp boat's engine was silent as well, and the only sounds Maggie heard were the hiss and pop of the flames and the lapping of the wake as it slapped at the sides of the boat.

"What the hell?" Wyatt asked, as he and Maggie walked to the starboard rail and looked at what they'd come for.

Maggie didn't recognize the old wooden skiff, and the name had been scratched or blasted off of the stern. But the lack of a name, and even the fact that it was on fire, weren't the details that stood out the most. The man hanging from the front of the cabin, and currently aflame, was more of an attention grabber.

"Now what?" Maggie asked.

"Well, we don't get too many Viking funerals around here," Wyatt said. "So I don't think it's that."

He grabbed one of the long metal fish hooks from its holder and poked at the burning skiff to keep them from bumping. Then he bent over sideways, to look up at the face.

Meanwhile, Dwight began looking like a cat with a hairball, and Wyatt heard him coughing into his hand.

"You all right, Dwight?" Wyatt asked.

"Yeah. Yeah, but, uh, the smell." Dwight gulped, looked away from the burning body. "I'm a vegetarian, you know?"

"Well, don't worry. We're not going to have to taste it."

Dwight took two steps to the port side and threw his beer up over the rail.

"Sorry," Wyatt said.

Maggie sniffed the air. Aside from the rather horrid odor of burning flesh, she could pick up no propane or other fuel that might have been used as an accelerant. That would help explain why it was burning so slowly.

"Well, that's kind of an interesting thing," Wyatt said, standing up.

"What is?" Maggie asked.

"That's Rupert Fain."

"What?"

Rupert Fain was the drug dealer that was suspected of blowing up her ex-husband on his shrimp boat at the town's 3rd of July celebration. They'd been looking for him since.

"It's Fain," Wyatt said, frowning. "I memorized his damn mug shot."

"He's from Gainesville. What's he doing out here?"

"Confirming the existence of karma, primarily."

⚓ ⚓ ⚓

The remainder of Maggie's and Wyatt's second date was attended not only by Dwight, two shrimpers and a burning dead guy, but also a dozen Coast Guard and assorted folks from the Sheriff's Office.

The fire was put out, the body brought aboard the Coast Guard cutter, and the oyster skiff, which had begun to sink, hauled ashore.

Terry Coyle was meeting the cutter at the marina in back of Sea-Fair Seafood, where the SO kept its boat. This would be his case, partly because he was, aside from Maggie, the only other Investigative Officer for the SO, and therefore on duty, and partly because Maggie wouldn't have been allowed to work the crime scene, anyway.

Rupert Fain was believed to have killed her ex-husband and she wasn't going to be allowed within twenty feet of the case.

Maggie docked her father's boat in its slip at Scipio Creek Marina, then she and Wyatt walked the half-block distance to the docks behind Sea-Fair. Dwight opted to skip a visit in favor of going home and inhaling a quantity of both Vick's and Budweiser.

Once she and Wyatt got to the docks, Maggie headed for the gurney on which the body of Rupert Fain was being placed.

"What are you doing?" Wyatt asked as he followed her.

"I just want to see," Maggie answered.

"See what? You already saw it out there," Wyatt said.

"I want to see his face."

"You have his mug shot on your desk," Wyatt countered. "I catch you looking at it all the time."

Maggie and Wyatt arrived among the group of EMTs and SO personnel near the gurney. Terry and the elderly medical examiner, Larry Davenport, were bending over the body.

"I want to look him in the face, Wyatt," Maggie said firmly.

Maggie could see enough of Fain's profile to know that his face was smoke-stained and perhaps just a little singed. Dirty-blond hair cut very short.

Larry was on the opposite side of the gurney from Maggie, and was inspecting the head. Maggie tried to peer around Terry's back to get a better look, but one of the EMTs was in her way, as well.

"No, I'd say he was already dead when he was set on fire," Larry was saying, peering over his bifocals. "One shot from what looks like it might be a .22, some small caliber, at any rate."

Larry turned the head so that the face was pointing toward Maggie. "No exit wound. Definitely a small caliber. I'd say it turned his brain straight to pudding, rattling around in there. Merciful, I suppose."

Maggie slapped the EMT on the waist, and he turned to look at her. "Hey, Bret," Maggie said. "Can you scoot over a little?"

He stepped aside just a bit and Maggie looked at the face of Rupert Fain, just a few feet away. He had a slightly surprised expression, and a neat bullet hole dead in the center of his forehead.

Maggie stood and looked at him for a long moment while Larry talked primarily to himself and secondarily to Terry. So this was the man.

This was the man they suspected of blowing up her ex-husband. Her kind and gentle ex-husband, who had made the mistake of getting into the pot transportation business when his shrimp boat was repossessed after the BP oil spill, and then made the mistake of getting out of the business just last month.

The prevailing theory, which she and Wyatt had refined over the last few weeks, was that Fain had suspected David of stealing about fifty-thousand dollars' worth of pot, and using the proceeds to buy himself a new boat. If so, he'd been mistaken. Wyatt had found bank statements proving that David had taken two years to painstakingly earn every penny he'd paid for the old wooden Jefferson trawler. What had happened to Fain's pot had yet to be discovered, but it didn't look like David had done anything other than deliver it.

The middleman between Fain and David had been found fried to a crisp in an old car in Gainesville a few weeks back, and David was dead two weeks later, blown up on his new boat in front of the ex-wife who still considered him her best friend.

Then someone had sent an ex-con named Charlie Harper to kill Maggie, too, a mission he'd failed in only because Wyatt had been on time for dinner.

Maggie knew it was a solid assumption on Wyatt's part, that Fain had sent Harper to kill her, and even that Harper had been the one to kill David. But Maggie had never told Wyatt what Harper had said before Wyatt showed up. Maggie had lain on the ground after being shot in the shoulder, and watched Harper walk toward her.

When he'd stopped a few feet away, he'd said, "I'm tired of cleaning up Boudreaux's messes." And that was a whole different kettle of fish. She wasn't too sure that Fain had sent Harper to kill her, but she was sure that Fain was responsible for the death of her ex-husband, the man she had loved since fifth grade.

Maggie bent over to get a closer look at Fain, looked into his dead brown eyes that even now looked small and shifty. She could feel everyone, particularly Wyatt, watching her.

"I hope you're grateful," Maggie said quietly. "I wouldn't have shot you first."

After telling Terry he'd read his report in the morning, Wyatt practically shoved Maggie toward the Scipio Creek docks. They walked for a few minutes without saying anything.

"This both complicates and simplifies my search for Fain somewhat," Wyatt finally said.

"Any ideas?" Maggie asked.

"Well, no," he said, sounding irritated about it. "You would be my first suspect, but you've screwed that up by being with me."

Maggie looked at him. "Oh come on, you wouldn't actually suspect me, would you?"

"Not really, no. You're not the vigilante type, but if you were, you wouldn't have let him off that easy."

They walked in silence the rest of the way to their cars. Wyatt leaned against his cruiser and Maggie leaned up against the passenger side door of her black Cherokee.

Wyatt glanced over at a couple of shrimpers who were heading out late. He and Maggie were in clear view of a few other people on the docks, as well as anyone on the deck at Up the Creek, the raw bar across the parking lot.

"There are probably a hundred people that wouldn't mind seeing Fain dead," Wyatt said. "He was a violent scumbag. But as far as I can tell, those hundred people are all in Gainesville. I can't think of one good reason for him to be dead here, instead of being dead there."

I'm tired of cleaning up Boudreaux's messes. It was Bennett Boudreaux who had pointed at Fain as a likely suspect for David's murder, or at least the contractor thereof. A few days later, the man who tried to kill her invoked Boudreaux's name.

"You don't have anything at all that might be a solid connection between Harper and Fain?" Maggie asked.

"No."

"Maybe I could look through the file. Maybe a fresh pair of eyes—"

"Your eyes, fresh or otherwise, will stay out of my case file," Wyatt said. "If there's anybody left to arrest for David's death, I'd like the charge to stick, not get thrown out of court because you were dragging your eyeballs across the documentation."

Maggie sighed. "I'm not implying that you're not doing a good job."

"I'm not inferring it, either," Wyatt said. "Nevertheless, you will stick to the foot and stay away from this one."

Wyatt was referring to the severed leg of Sport Wilmette, which was pulled up out of the ocean in a shrimper's net a few days before David's death. Wilmette *was* Maggie's case, though he probably shouldn't be. She didn't remember ever meeting the man, but she had learned during the investigation that they shared one terrible moment in their histories, one that made her investigation of his death unethical. One that she hadn't shared with Wyatt.

She shrugged that line of thought off, needing to spend more time thinking about it before she decided what kind of person she was to withhold the information, especially from this man who was her close friend and quite possibly the second man she would love in her lifetime.

"Okay, I'll stick with the foot," she said. "Hey, I get the stitches out and the sling off tomorrow.'

"Already? Geez. Used to be, you got shot you were in the hospital for weeks," Wyatt said. "Now, they boot you out of the hospital the next day and yank your stitches out a week later."

"Two weeks," Maggie said.

"Whatever." Wyatt looked back over toward the docks. One of the shrimpers raised a hand in greeting, and Wyatt raised one back, then sighed, arms folded across his chest. "I bet clandestine romance is simpler in Orlando."

"I'm not moving to Orlando just so we can go unnoticed," she said, smiling.

"You still haven't cooked me that dinner," he said. "Maybe we should do that for our third attempt at a second date."

"Let's do that," she said.

They looked at each other for a minute and Maggie wished that Wyatt wasn't her boss and her children's father wasn't dead. That she hadn't started keeping so many secrets.

"Well, okee-doke," Wyatt said, opening his car door. "Pretend I kissed you goodnight."

Maggie smiled as he started the car. "Pretend I liked it."

Wyatt laughed sarcastically. "You're just adorable. We both know your knees were knocking."

Maggie watched him drive off, her smile fading. Too many secrets.

CHAPTER

The next morning, Maggie went to the doctor to get her stitches out, which she endured with an embarrassing amount of wincing, mewing and gasping, at least for someone who carried a Glock.

Afterward, she was desperate for coffee, and longed to get a *café con leche* from the restaurant of the same name, but she hadn't been there in weeks. It was right across from Riverfront Park, where David had been killed, and she hadn't been able to bring herself to go back yet.

Instead, she drove over to Delores's Sweet Shoppe, a local institution and Maggie's second-favorite coffee spot. She needed a little extra down time after her harrowing experience, so she ordered her coffee to drink there, sat down at one of the little round tables, and practiced using her right hand again.

She was on her second cup of coffee, and contemplating ordering another to go, when a slightly raised voice from near the counter got her attention.

"Oh, it's the little sheriff!"

She looked up to see William and Robert, who owned the local flower shop, descending on her in a quiet flurry, to-go cups of coffee in hand.

"We need to talk to you about this newest nonsense," William said, sliding into the chair across from her. He was in his early fifties or so, short and slight, with golden hair that couldn't possibly be natural but looked good anyway.

Before Maggie could answer, Robert, much larger, a few years younger and with slick black hair, slid into the chair beside William and nodded.

"Complete nonsense," he said in a hushed voice.

"I'm sorry, what do you mean?" Maggie asked.

"The burning boat guy," William said in a stage whisper.

"Completely uncalled for," Robert said.

"How do you know about this?" Maggie asked, and immediately felt stupid for the knee-jerk response. There were fewer than three thousand people living in Apalach. Everybody knew everything.

"It's in this morning's paper," Robert said.

"Front page," William added. "Do you not read the paper?"

Robert put a hand on William's wrist. "Rude. She doesn't need the paper, she has a police radio."

William flicked his hand off and looked back at Maggie. "What on God's green earth is going on?"

Maggie put her coffee cup down. "Well, it's not my case, so I really couldn't say."

"This is not a useful occurrence in the middle of summer," William said. "First your foot, and now a burning boat man."

"It's very bad for business," Robert said. "Yours is good, ours is bad."

"I'm sorry," Maggie said.

"Who wants to come down on vacation if they have to worry about being chopped into pieces or burned at the stake?" William said, almost whispering.

"Well, he wasn't exactly—"

"Not to be impolite, but whatever," William said. "Some guy was out on the Bay doing his Joan of Arc impression and the tourists are going to be taken aback for sure."

"They're gonna rethink," Robert said.

"Those talentless hacks in Destin—" He looked at Robert. "Who are those people?"

Robert gave him a dismissive wave. "Bountiful Buds."

William looked back at Maggie with a pinched mouth. "Sounds like they're selling beer. Anyway, the tourists will be in Destin, getting all their bouquets from those hussies, and we'll be on the longest smoke break in florist history."

"I'm sure Sheriff Hamilton and the rest of the department will be bringing the case to a quick close," Maggie said. "And I doubt too many people outside of Apalach are reading our paper this morning."

"Oh, you don't know," Robert said. "Those vacation rental people, they read it online, check the weather and whatnot."

"They look for shark reports and early bird coupons," William explained.

Maggie took another swallow of her coffee and picked up her keys, hoping to look like she really needed to be off. "Listen, you guys, I'm really sorry, but it'll be okay," she started.

"And what about the foot, anyway?" Robert asked. "We're still waiting for the other shoe to drop on that one."

William slapped at Robert's wrist.

"No, really," Robert said. "We keep expecting more pieces to wash up on the beach or something."

"Or for some pelican to yak up an elbow in front of The Soda Fountain," said William.

"Guys, the rest of that body is long gone," Maggie said, and jingled her keys to signify her being needed somewhere that wasn't there. "We're not going to find anything else."

She stood up and pulled her purse onto her shoulder.

"I'll tell you what. I'll go straight to the office right now and see what we've learned about the man in the boat, okay?"

William and Robert stood up. "Oh, good," William said. "And let me tell you something, we will give you free weekly arrangements for life if you people would just keep any subsequent serial killer activity quiet."

"Nice arrangements," Robert said.

"These cases have nothing to do with each other," Maggie said. "There's no serial killer."

"Three whacked out murders in like three weeks—" William started, then gasped as Robert slapped him on the shoulder.

Maggie swallowed and tried to smile.

"I'm so sorry," William said in a pained whisper.

Maggie started away from the table. "It's okay," she said. "But I really need to go."

As she opened the front door, she heard Robert back by the table.

"Why are you retarded?" he asked William rhetorically.

⚓ ⚓ ⚓

A few blocks across town, in the Historic District, Bennett Boudreaux sat in the sunny kitchen of his Low Country Plantation-style home. He stirred some milk and sugar into his second cup of chicory coffee, as Amelia, the lanky, middle-aged Creole woman he'd brought with him from Louisiana, stood at the island, watching over the one slice of bacon in her skillet.

Boudreaux was a strikingly handsome man, even in his early sixties, with a thick head of brown hair just lightly touched with silver above his ears. Though he was just a little over five-seven, his trim physique and commanding presence made him seem like a larger, younger man. For most people, though, it was Boudreaux's eyes that caught attention. They were piercing and magnetic, and an incredible shade of blue.

Though he was well-educated and impeccably-mannered, there was a darkness and a blue-collar foundation to Boudreaux that intimidated most people, even the ones who didn't know who he was.

Boudreaux took a sip of his coffee, then started eating his dry toast.

"I appreciate you don't start with her this mornin'," Amelia said.

"I never start with her," Boudreaux said quietly.

"Who are you tellin'?" Amelia carefully flipped the bacon with a pair of tongs. "She was up half the night, trying to find Johnny Carson on the TV."

"He's dead."

"Don't say nothin' to her about that. I already argued myself to death with her."

"Maybe we need to start slipping something into her chamomile tea," Boudreaux said. "To help her sleep."

"Maybe you need to start slippin' somethin' into mine," Amelia said. "She don't sleep, I don't sleep."

Boudreaux looked over at Amelia. She looked younger than she actually was, but her shoulders were beginning to slump and there were grayish circles beneath her eyes.

"Maybe it's time to hire someone else to come in here and cook and clean. You just take care of her."

Amelia put a hand on her hip and looked at him. "Ain't nobody comin' in here, takin' my job."

"You'd still have a job. Taking care of your mother."

"Who gonna fix your food? You think you gonna find someone 'round here makes étouffée? You'd starve to death, then she'd cut my throat."

Boudreaux sighed. "Why do the two of you make everything difficult? Hire somebody to clean and cook for Lily, and you can still cook for the three of us. Disaster averted."

Amelia picked up the slice of bacon and laid it on a small plate on which sat one over-medium egg and one slice of wheat toast. "Herself still be runnin' me all 'round, playin' Steppin Fetchit."

"You don't work for Lily, you work for me," Boudreaux said. He unwrapped the weekly *Apalachicola Times* that sat beside his plate.

"She gon' complain 'bout somebody new."

"Then shoot her," he said mildly.

"I do it, me."

"I'd give you a raise," he said.

He opened the paper and the picture below the front page headline took his attention away from the conversation at hand. It was a small oyster skiff, mostly burned, being towed by a Coast Guard cutter. His first thought was that one of the oystermen had had an accident, but then he started reading.

He got far enough to find out that the boat had been found burning in the middle of the bay the night before, with a man's body lashed to the cabin. Then the back door opened, and Miss Evangeline's aluminum walker clattered through, Miss Evangeline not quite hot on its heels.

Miss Evangeline was well over ninety and well under five feet tall. While Amelia was tall and large-boned, her mother was tiny and had the bones of a sparrow. She wore a red bandana wrapped around her head, and a red-checked housedress that had started out too big for her, then grown enormous as she shrank. Her eyes, magnified a hundred times behind her thick glasses, were the largest thing about her.

Boudreaux stood up, walked around the table, and pulled out Miss Evangeline's chair.

"Mornin', Mama," Amelia said.

"Mornin', baby," Miss Evangeline said, her voice like two pieces of paper being rubbed together.

Boudreaux waited by her chair while Miss Evangeline undertook to reach it, her walker thumping along softly on its tennis balls. Miss Evangeline had been Boudreaux's nanny when he was a child in Louisiana, then become his housekeeper and cook when he was grown. In her mind, she'd never stopped being his nanny. It would be embarrassing, if people were privy to their relationship, given his status as the town crime lord.

"Good morning, Miss Evangeline," he said as she reached the table. He kissed her on both cheeks, then held her chair as she sat.

"I don' know yet, me," she said.

Boudreaux went back to his chair and sat down, then poured his third cup of coffee from the fancy flowered pot. Amelia set her mother's plate and a cup of tea in front of her, then went back to the island to start cleaning up.

Miss Evangeline stared across the table at Boudreaux as he added milk to his coffee.

"I need you change the batt'ry on my buzzer," she said. "He dead again."

Boudreaux reached for his paper. "It's not the batteries, it's you," he said. "It may surprise you to learn that normal people use a newspaper to kill Palmetto bugs, not a Taser."

Amelia let out a heavy sigh over by the sink, as Miss Evangeline stopped stirring her tea and stared at Boudreaux, the sunlight flashing off her thick lenses. She poked her tongue around in her mouth for a moment before she spoke.

"You in the mood to sass me today, then," she said.

"No, I'm just advising you that your aim's not good enough to keep those batteries alive for more than a day," he said mildly as he read.

"Big cockroach slap themself all over my window screens all night, come in my house run 'round like they my housecats. I buzz they eyeballs out, me."

"Well, then don't gripe about your dead batteries," Boudreaux said distractedly as he read the article. Miss Evangeline set about painstakingly cutting her egg into hundredths.

When he turned to the second page, Boudreaux read that Rupert Fain was the man found in the burning boat.

He needed to give that some thought. Then he needed to talk to Maggie Redmond.

He'd told Maggie that Rupert Fain was the most likely candidate for her ex-husband's murder, and he'd believed it to be true. He'd known Fain had been robbed of the last shipment of pot that David had delivered to Fain's middleman, Myron Graham, because his stepson, Patrick had told him. Patrick had known, because he liked to use his power as the Assistant State's Attorney to finagle "commissions" out of people like Myron.

It wasn't until later that Patrick had almost proudly admitted that he'd been the one who stole Fain's pot, and that he'd actually been the one to kill Myron in the process. Then he'd let Maggie's ex-husband take the fall for it.

Boudreaux might kill someone who needed killing, but he didn't kill over money and he didn't let other people die on his behalf, either. He'd liked and respected David, and he'd been happy for him when he'd gotten out of running pot and gotten himself a new boat. Patrick had intentionally let David take the fall for something he himself had done, and Boudreaux despised it.

But Patrick was still his stepson. Boudreaux and Lily had married back in Louisiana, purely for business and social reasons, when Patrick was four and Craig was barely a year old. Lily got the financial security she wanted and Boudreaux got her family's social and political connections, something not often afforded the son of an oysterman, even one who had built a multi-million dollar business.

Boudreaux sighed and stared at words he was no longer reading. This was messy. He didn't like messes.

"What that burnin' in the paper?" Miss Evangeline asked, peering across the table at the front page.

"Trouble," Boudreaux answered.

"Who trouble?"

"I'm not sure yet."

He stirred coffee that didn't need stirring and the kitchen was silent for a moment, save for Amelia's loading of the dishwasher and Miss Evangeline's dentures clicking together as she nibbled at her egg. Boudreaux picked the paper back up and tried to think.

"I need you get me another television set," she said.

Boudreaux lowered the paper and looked at her. "What did you do to the television?"

"I didn't do nothin', me. It broke. Don't have Johnny Carson channel no more."

Boudreaux glanced over at Amelia as she clanged some pots together at the sink, then he looked back at Miss Evangeline. "Are you thinking they just took NBC right off the TV?"

"Don't know what they do, but I don't have no Johnny Carson."

Boudreaux lifted his paper back up. His heart wasn't really in it, but he couldn't just let it go.

"Maybe Walter Cronkite will say something about it on the news tonight," he said mildly.

THREE

The Sheriff's Office was in Eastpoint, an even smaller town than Apalach, located across the causeway that traversed Scipio Creek and the mouth of the bay.

When Maggie got there, she poked her head into Wyatt's office. He looked like he'd been there a while.

"Hey," she said.

He looked up from his computer monitor and sighed. "Hey back," he said.

"How's it going?"

"It's going," he answered. "Between us, Terry and I have amassed quite a collection of people who would love to see Fain dead. It's just that none of them are here."

"Sure they are," Maggie said. "Every shrimper and oysterman in Franklin County. Everybody loved David."

"Good point."

"I'm not offering that as a viable lead, I'm just saying."

"I know." He took off his SO ball cap and ran a hand through his hair, then pointed at her arm. "You got your arm back."

"Yeah." She looked down at her arm and shrugged. "I was kind of a baby about it. Embarrassing."

"So what are you working on today?" he asked her, slapping his cap back on.

"Not a lot. I have a lot of paperwork to catch up on, and I need to close the case file on the Kleins. Then, you know, the foot."

"Yeah, the foot." Wyatt leaned back in his leather chair. "What's going on with it?"

Maggie looked at him for a few seconds, then shrugged. "I'm working on something. I'll get back to you."

He took a long drink of the gigantic bottle of Mountain Dew on his desk, watching her as he did.

"You do that," he said quietly.

Maggie felt something skitter along like a spider inside her chest. Keeping secrets was bad enough; the idea that Wyatt might know something was amiss was even more upsetting.

"I will," she said. "I'll let you get back to it."

"Okay," he said.

Maggie walked down the hall to her office, wondering if the way she felt was anything like the way criminals felt when they knew she was watching them.

⚓   ⚓   ⚓

Maggie spent most of the day on paperwork that had piled up over the last few weeks, between investigating the case of Sport Wilmette's foot, what happened with David, and her injury. Once she got caught up, she busied herself with cleaning her desk while she thought about whether and how to come clean with Wyatt about her connection to Gregory Boudreaux and Sport Wilmette, and her theory about what had happened to Sport.

During the course of her day, she either picked up or reached for her phone several times, to call Bennett Boudreaux. For whatever reason, and she chose not to consider it too carefully, she never made the call.

It was with some surprise, then, that she saw Boudreaux's number on her screen when her cell phone rang late in the afternoon.

"Hello?" she answered.

"Hello, Maggie," Boudreaux said.

"Hello, Mr. Boudreaux."

"I need to speak with you," he said politely. "I was wondering if you could meet me."

"When?"

"Today."

"What's it about?" she asked.

"The front page of the paper."

"That's not my case," Maggie answered. "He either killed David or had David killed. I can't have anything to do with it."

"I'm sure that's true... professionally."

Maggie wasn't sure what to say to that. She wanted to talk to him, too, and some of what she needed to discuss involved Fain. But, the idea that he wanted to speak with her about it kind of threw her.

"Maggie, I would appreciate it very much if you would come talk with me," he said quietly.

"Okay, Mr. Boudreaux," she said. "Now?"

"That would be nice," he said.

"Where would you like me to meet you?"

⚓ ⚓ ⚓

A few minutes later, Maggie leaned on Wyatt's door jamb and waited while he finished up a conversation with one of the deputies. Once the deputy had left, Maggie walked into the office, pulling her purse up on her shoulder.

"Hey," Wyatt said. "You heading out?"

"Yeah." Maggie glanced into the hallway before going on. "Hey, I was wondering if I could talk to you about something."

Wyatt tilted his head just a bit. "Sure. What's up?"

Maggie looked back toward the door. "It's kind of private."

"Work private?"

"Mostly."

"Stop skulking by the door. Come over here."

Maggie walked over to stand near Wyatt's desk, as he tossed an empty Mountain Dew into the trash and grabbed another one out of the mini-fridge behind him.

"You know, those things have flame retardant in them."

"I know. That's why I've never spontaneously combusted," he said, cracking it open. "And I have a factoid for you, too. If you try any harder to look like we're not talking about anything, people are going to start wondering why we're not talking about anything."

Maggie sighed. "I'm just trying to be careful," she said quietly. "And it is private."

"Okay." Wyatt lowered his voice, despite what he'd just said. "You wanna come by the house later?"

When Maggie thought of Wyatt's house, she thought of sitting on his dock on their first date, or of falling asleep in his arms on the couch after she'd finally let herself feel David's death. If Wyatt was going to be upset with her, she didn't want it to be there.

"Actually, can you come out to mine?"

"Sure. What about the kids?" he asked.

"They're going over to my parents' to spend the night," she said.

Maggie expected one of Wyatt's eyebrow dances and a smart remark. She didn't get one. Instead, his eyes narrowed just a little.

"Okay."

"I need to follow up on something with the foot first," Maggie said. "About seven okay?"

"Yeah, I'll be there."

"Okay," Maggie said, feeling uncomfortable with the way he was looking at her. "Well."

"If you get shot this time, I'm not coming over there anymore."

Maggie let out a nervous laugh and headed for the door. "I'll try to avoid it."

⚓ ⚓ ⚓

Lafayette Park was located on the bay, in a residential neighborhood just off the Historic District. Wyatt's cottage was just a few blocks away and, as Maggie passed it, she wondered if she'd be as welcome there after tonight.

She parked in the small parking area on 13th Street and turned off the Jeep, took a deep breath. She could see a couple of children playing in the big white gazebo in the center of the park, where local couples liked to have their wedding photos taken. Two young mothers stood nearby, and through her open window, Maggie could just hear one of them call to one or more of the kids. The wind had picked up considerably since earlier in the day, and a sheet of dark, gray clouds looked low enough to touch.

Maggie rolled up her window and got out of the car. She could see Boudreaux, sitting on a bench that looked out toward the bay. Her hiking boots thumped dully on the brick-paver path that led there.

Boudreaux looked over his shoulder as she got nearer, then stood up and waited for her as she walked over to the bench. The wind ruffled his hair, and he ran a hand through it to get it out of his eyes.

"Hello, Maggie," he said.

"Hello, Mr. Boudreaux."

As she always was, Maggie was struck by how attractive he was. It had partly to do with his features, especially those intense blue eyes, but it had as much to do with his combination of roughness and casual elegance.

His light blue linen shirt and cream-colored slacks cost more than Maggie's entire wardrobe, and she could probably take a decent vacation if she pawned his watch, but his deeply tanned skin was that of a man who had spent his life on the water, and his hands were those of an oysterman, with calloused palms and fingers that bore small white scars from rock and shell.

"There's no one out on the pier. I thought we might walk out there," he said.

Maggie nodded, and he held a hand out toward the long pier that extended into the bay. He fell into step with her as they walked across the back of the park toward the pier.

"I appreciate you meeting me," he said politely.

"Actually, I was planning on calling you," Maggie said.

"Is that right?' he asked, looking over at her with those inquisitive eyes. "Well, serendipity."

The young mothers were herding their children toward Avenue B at the front of the park, leaving Maggie and Boudreaux alone. Maggie got the faint taste of wet metal in her mouth as she breathed, and thunder rumbled quietly in the distance, over the sea.

"My timing may not have been perfect," Boudreaux said. "I apologize. I'm afraid I don't have an umbrella."

"I don't actually own one," Maggie said.

"Neither do I," he said, and looked at her with a small smile. "That's right. You like the storms as much as I do."

"Yes," she said.

They stepped onto the thousand foot long pier, which had been badly damaged by Hurricane Dennis in 2005, then rebuilt in 2008. It was a popular place for locals to fish, but not today. Their feet thumped softly on the wood as they walked, accompanied by the sound of the sea oats and tall grass on either side as they rustled in the wind.

"How's your arm, by the way?"

"Much better, thank you," Maggie answered.

They walked in silence for a moment before Boudreaux spoke again. "I was very upset to hear what happened, Maggie," he said.

Maggie wasn't sure what she wanted to say to that, so she said nothing.

"This man that shot you. I understand he was from East-point?"

"Yes, at least, recently. He was originally from Fort Lauderdale."

"And have you tracked him back to Rupert Fain?"

"Like I said earlier, Mr. Boudreaux, it's not my case," Maggie said. "I'm actually not privy to all that much. But no, we haven't exactly connected him to Fain."

Boudreaux looked over at her, then looked out at the water. "I find that troubling."

Maggie wondered if it bothered him for the same reason it bothered her.

"So do I," she finally said.

She'd spent so much time wondering whether to confront Boudreaux about the man that shot her that the idea of walking away from this conversation without doing it made her feel tired.

"Mr. Boudreaux, do you remember a few days after I was shot, I asked you if you had tried to hurt me?"

He looked her in the eye. "Yes, I do. And I assured you that I hadn't. Why do you mention it?"

Maggie didn't think the way she felt was too typical of someone confronting someone about whether or not they had tried to kill her. Instead, it felt more like fear of disappointment.

"The man that shot me. Charlie Harper. After he shot me, he walked over to finish me off. He said something to me."

"What was that?" Boudreaux asked.

Maggie stopped walking and turned to face him. He stopped as well and waited.

Maggie took a deep breath through her nose, trying to look like she wasn't. "He said 'I'm tired of cleaning up Boudreaux's messes.'"

The change in Boudreaux's expression wasn't significant, but it was noticeable. His eyes narrowed just fractionally, and Maggie saw a vein in his neck pop, as though he were clenching his teeth. She watched him as he took a long, slow breath and let it out just as slowly.

"I didn't send him to hurt you, Maggie," he said quietly. "You are asking again, are you not?"

"I guess I am," she answered.

He started walking again, and she followed. They didn't speak again until they reached the covered area at the end of the dock. The wind was stronger there, and whipped at Maggie's hair, pulling strands of it from its clip and lashing her face with them. She ignored it and watched Boudreaux as he put his hands on the wooden rail and looked out at the bay.

She and Boudreaux had been playing some kind of verbal hide and seek for weeks, ever since she'd been called

to the beach over on the island, to investigate the suicide of his nephew, Gregory. She'd lived her entire life in
Apalach and talked to Boudreaux maybe ten times in all
those years, and never anything beyond "hello." She'd never even worked a case involving him, though there had
been several.

Suddenly, they were conversing over oysters on the
deck at Boss Oyster, playing some sort of cat and mouse
with the truth about her and Gregory. He'd let her know,
without coming out and saying it, that he knew Gregory
had raped her when she was a teen. She'd always felt that
he suspected she may have killed him. She'd also worried
about how he felt about that. He was known for being a
vengeful enemy and fiercely protective of family.

But, for reasons she really didn't want to look at too
closely, she had a certain respect for Boudreaux. She even
liked him, when she had the guts to admit that to herself.
Even more troubling, she wanted his apparent approval of
her to be genuine. She could handle someone wanting to
kill her; she just didn't want it to be Boudreaux.

Boudreaux turned around and leaned back against the
rail, looked at her again.

"I think we have arrived at the point I predicted we
would sooner or later," he said.

"Which point is that?"

"Well, if I ask you what reason you think I have for
wanting to hurt you, your answer is inevitably going to
bring us to other questions you have in your head, but haven't asked."

"Would you answer them if I did?" she asked, but she
already knew that he would. She'd always known that he
was waiting for her to ask.

"Yes."

Maggie's heart started beating a little harder in her chest, and there seemed to be less oxygen in the air. She got as much of it as she could before speaking again.

"You know that Gregory raped me, don't you?" The words felt like a foreign language. She'd never even said it out loud to herself.

Boudreaux's left eye twitched almost imperceptibly. "Yes," he said quietly.

No one knew what had happened when she was fifteen, except for a psychologist she had visited three times in her twenties. Therefore, no one she knew had ever looked at her with that knowledge in their eyes, and it struck her as surreal that this man would be the first to do so. Not her parents, not her ex-husband, but Bennett Boudreaux, Apalach's own alleged crime lord, and a man she hadn't even known until last month.

"Have you always known?" she asked.

"No," he answered. "I knew nothing about it until the night before he died."

Maggie looked out at the water a moment, trying to gather her thoughts, to marshal her questions now that she was asking them. "He told you?"

Boudreaux sighed. "He asked me to go over there because he wanted money. To go to South America. You were one of the reasons why. Apparently, seeing you around town, when he was here, made him feel a lot of guilt. Something he wasn't very comfortable with."

Maggie restrained herself from mentioning that she'd never been very happy seeing Gregory around town, either.

He looked out at the water for a moment, then looked back at her. "He showed me the letter he wrote you."

The letter. An apology from Gregory, which had arrived in her mail the day of his funeral. Getting it had messed with her head. When she'd found out that Sport Wilmette, the owner of the foot, was an old friend of Gregory's, she'd assumed that he'd sent the letter.

"Did you send me that letter?" she asked.

"Yes."

"Why, dammit?" she snapped.

He looked surprised. Surprised and angry. "Because he owed you a damned apology," he said evenly.

"Do you know what it was like to get it after he was dead?" she asked. "It would have been a shock when he was alive, but the day of his funeral?"

"I'm sorry. I really didn't consider that."

Maggie watched a gull dive into the water near the grass, watched it take off again a moment later. She needed a break from Boudreaux's gaze. When she was ready she looked back at him.

"Do you think I killed Gregory?" she asked.

"No, I don't. He shot himself."

Maggie let out a deep sigh. She'd had that question weighing so heavily on her mind for so long that she felt almost weightless without it. Not relieved, just suddenly unburdened.

"There was someone else there that day. In the woods. I never saw him," she said. "It was Wilmette, wasn't it?" Boudreaux had hinted as much during her investigation, but she wanted to hear it.

"Yes," he said flatly.

"You said he asked you for money, to invest in some business. Was he trying to blackmail you?"

"I'm sure he thought of it as something else."

"He wasn't in much of a position to tell anyone."

"I don't think he thought it through," Boudreaux said. "I told you. He was dumber than hell."

Maggie was a little surprised that her next question was harder to ask than the previous one. She knew it was because she wanted him to answer "no," but he would probably say "yes," and she didn't know what she would have to with that.

"Did you kill him for it?"

Boudreaux had freely admitted that Wilmette had been at his seafood business, Sea-Fair, the night before he'd gone missing. The place where he'd just built a fish processing room, complete with knives and stainless steel tables, and hoses for washing blood down the drains in the floor. And, a few nights after Wilmette had last been seen, she'd run into Boudreaux at Boss Oyster. He'd been on his way out to do some "night fishing." A few days after that, poor Axel Blackwell dragged Wilmette's foot up in his shrimp net.

She watched Boudreaux now, as he watched her. Then he scratched gently at his left eyebrow, something she'd come to know he did when he was thinking about what to say. She waited.

"I'm going to answer your question in a way that's meant to protect you more than it is me," he said. "Hypothetically, if I had killed him, it wouldn't have been because of some ridiculous attempt to blackmail me with public embarrassment. I manage my public reputation fairly well, given what many people already know about me."

"What would the reason have been? If you had killed him?"

"It would have been because the pathetic excuse for a man stood by and watched a fifteen year old girl get brutalized."

Maggie smelled moldy oak leaves and damp soil, heard the disgusting rhythm of Gregory Boudreaux's breathing, and couldn't stop her head from twitching just a little toward her shoulder. She swallowed a faint sense of nausea and had to look away for a moment.

"And you think the penalty for rape should be death?" she asked him finally.

"Don't you?" he asked gently.

She didn't know how to answer that. She wasn't sorry that either man was dead. She folded her arms across her chest. She didn't want to talk anymore about the subject. She was unused to it, and its foreignness left her feeling cold and unprotected.

"Did you kill Fain?"

"Did I kill Fain?" he asked, surprised. "Am I now under suspicion for every homicide that takes place?"

She didn't answer him. He sighed and almost smiled.

"To be honest, I asked you to meet me because I thought maybe you had," he said.

"Me?"

"It crossed my mind, yes."

"I was with Wyatt and Deputy Dwight Shultz when that boat was set on fire."

"But it *was* set on fire," he said.

"What's your point?" she asked.

"If you want a shoot a drug dealer, you do it and be done with it," he said. "You don't bother with symbolism."

"Well, I didn't do it."

"Clearly," he said. "But it seems to me that someone tried to make it look like you might have, someone who didn't know you'd have such a good alibi. I could amend that by saying someone tried to make it look like *one* of us might have done it."

"Why would someone think that you would be a likely suspect?"

"You suspected me."

"That's because…" Maggie trailed off, shaking her head.

"Because of what?"

"Because of this…weird relationship we have going on," she said, not finding the words that felt more accurate.

"Well, but we're not the only people who know about that, are we?" he asked mildly. "People have seen us at Boss, they saw you dance with me at the festival. They might not know the nature of our relationship, but there are quite a few theories going around."

Maggie nodded slightly and then shook her head.

"What's Wyatt's theory? I'm sure he has one."

"That you want me on your payroll," she answered.

"Well, you and I have already cleared that up."

"What is your interest, Mr. Boudreaux?" Maggie asked tiredly.

"It started because you were wronged, horribly, by someone in my family," he answered. "Now I just like you."

He held up a hand, though she hadn't been ready to say anything. "It's nothing romantic, I assure you, although that theory's been bandied about as well."

It had never actually occurred to Maggie that his interest would be sexual, and if the rest of their conversation wasn't so upsetting, she would have laughed.

"Did you know Charlie Harper, Mr. Boudreaux?"

"No. I'd never heard of him until I saw his name in the paper."

"Why would he mention your name?"

"I don't know the answer to that question, Maggie. But I didn't send him."

Maggie didn't know if she really believed him, or if she just felt like she did because she wanted to.

"I can't keep all this from Wyatt anymore," she said. "I can't keep working the Wilmette case. I never should have handled your nephew's case. I'm going to have to tell Wyatt about my connection with them."

"Do you need to do that for professional reasons or personal ones?"

"Both."

"You care for him. Wyatt."

Denial was on the tip of her tongue, but who was *he* going to tell? "Yes," she said simply.

Boudreaux nodded. "Good."

They looked at each other a moment, then he broke the silence. "Do what you need to do, Maggie. We'll let the chips fall where they may. I'm a lot more careful than old Sport was."

For just a moment, Maggie felt a flash of protectiveness for Boudreaux. It confused and upset her, and she needed time and space. Space that he wasn't in.

"I need to go," she said shortly. "I'm sorry. Goodnight, Mr. Boudreaux."

"Goodnight, Maggie."

Maggie turned and walked back the way they'd come. After a few steps, though, she stopped and turned around. He was still leaning against the rail, watching her.

"For the record, I want it to be true," she said.

"For what to be true?" he asked.

"That you didn't try to hurt me."

Boudreaux smiled, almost sadly. "I like that you want that."

Maggie didn't know why she'd felt the urge to tell him that. And she was tired to death of wondering why she felt and did and said too many things concerning Boudreaux. She headed for the park again. Halfway up the pier, fat drops of rain began to fall, *thunking* against the wood in accompaniment to her footsteps.

She didn't find the rain as comforting as she usually did.

CHAPTER

FOUR

Maggie turned onto the dirt drive that served her property, stopped the Jeep long enough to get out and grab the mail from the mailbox, then headed for the house.

Maggie's dirt road was at the end of a road that ran north out of town for a few miles, angling toward the Apalachicola River, then stopped dead for no apparent reason. Her nearest neighbors were half a mile through the woods, and her little stilt house, built by her grandfather of cypress as strong as stone, sat on a promontory at the back of her five acres, which meant she could see the river from both her side and her back decks.

It was a secluded place, with a dozen chickens, a big raised bed garden, and an old dock where she kept her Grandpa's oyster skiff and a small aluminum bass boat. It was simple, but Maggie's father had been raised there and now she was raising her kids there and she didn't want to be anywhere else.

Maggie pulled into the gravel turnaround in front of the house and parked. By the time she climbed out of the Jeep, her Catahoula Parish Leopard hound, Coco, was already coming down the deck stairs at a speed that looked more like suicide than descent. She wasn't even halfway down when Stoopid appeared from somewhere under the house.

Stoopid was an Ameraucana rooster of diminutive size, but always seemed to have a great weight on his shoulders. He managed not to be trampled by Coco as he ran at Maggie, wings and neck feathers in full deployment, to advise her that it was getting dark, or that he had spotted her, or that it was raining. His messages usually tended to be vague, but urgent.

Coco arrived at Maggie first and commenced disassembling herself at Maggie's feet, and Stoopid, who had a nervous condition, veered off at the last minute, giving Maggie one of his knock-off crows as he flung himself toward the chicken yard.

"Hey, baby," Maggie said, as she rubbed Coco's belly, then she headed up the stairs, Coco jingling and grinning behind her.

Maggie set her purse and the mail down on the old cypress dining table just inside the front door. The dining area and living area were one open room, which the storm clouds had made darker than it usually was at this hour in the summer, but the kids had left one lamp burning on the side table.

Maggie and Coco walked down the short hallway off of the living room, and Maggie quickly peeled off her clothes and climbed into the shower. Her conversation with Boudreaux had made a shower seem even more necessary than it usually did at the end of the day.

Once she'd run the hot water empty, Maggie changed into clean khaki shorts and a white tee shirt, and poured herself a glass of Muscadine wine. She took a decent swallow of it before carrying it through the living room and the sliding glass door out to the deck. Coco, tags clinking, settled down beside Maggie as she sat down at the small round table.

Maggie had begun to calm halfway through her shower, and she'd managed to quiet her mind to the point that she could think.

She'd always been good, sometimes too good, at compartmentalizing her feelings. Though affectionate and warm by nature, it was very easy for her to put away feelings that overwhelmed her, be they fear or anxiety or anger.

It was an aftereffect of the rape that she considered some small recompense for the occasional flashback or nightmare. Some people would consider it a symptom; she considered it a tool.

Maggie couldn't help believing in her gut that Boudreaux had been honest with her about Charlie Harper. On the ride home, and in the shower, she had replayed Boudreaux's words and expressions and, even though she was always wary of believing something she wanted to believe, she felt he was telling the truth.

She'd turned Charlie Harper's words around and around in her head, contrasting them with what she felt in her gut to be true. What she'd finally decided was that Fain had known somehow that Boudreaux had pointed suspicion toward him, and that, in doing so, he had created a "mess." As far as any prior messes, Maggie didn't really care.

She was on her second glass of wine, which she was drinking more slowly, when Wyatt pulled into the yard and parked next to Maggie's Cherokee. Coco's backside vibrated on the planks of the deck, and she accidentally let out a small squeal, like a kid letting a little bit of helium out of a balloon.

"Go ahead," Maggie said, and Coco bolted for the stairs.

Maggie walked to the top of the deck stairs and watched as Coco excitedly greeted Wyatt, who bent down and gave her a rub before heading for the stairs. He nearly trod upon Stoopid, who had barreled out to advise him of something important.

"Geez, Stoopid, take a Xanax," he mumbled as he headed for the stairs. He looked up and saw Maggie. "Hey," he said, as he started up.

"Hey," Maggie said.

Wyatt had showered, and his hair was still a bit damp. She noticed his impressively thick mustache looked freshly trimmed. He was wearing faded jeans and a white button down shirt with the sleeves rolled up and the tails out. She thought he was perhaps the most casually handsome man she'd ever met, and she wished this was their second date. For just a moment, she considered changing her plans for the evening.

Wyatt stopped a couple of steps below her, which put them eye to eye. He put a hand on either stair rail.

"So, I was thinking," he said. "Whatever it is you want to talk about, I already know it's not good, so why don't we go ahead and have a nice kiss and a hug now, in case one or both of us doesn't feel like it later? Unless, what you want to tell me is that you've decided to skip this whole thing with us."

"No. Of course not," she said quietly.

"Well, then brace yourself," he said.

He slipped an arm around her waist and tugged her to him, then kissed her. It was warm and gentle and firm, and becoming very familiar. She'd known him very well for six years, but in recent weeks he had become familiar in completely new ways. The way his wavy brown hair felt between her fingers, the way his lips felt, how he tasted faintly of brown sugar.

For her entire life, Maggie had loved a man who was slightly built and only stood five nine. The first time Wyatt had held her, it had felt like visiting a foreign country. Now, he was beginning to feel a little bit like home. She would have liked to have enjoyed the moment more, but there was a weight of dread in her chest that kept her from it.

Wyatt took his mouth from hers, gave her a quick kiss on the neck, then straightened up and bounced on the step, which trembled and creaked beneath him. "You need to fix this thing," he said, frowning.

"Yeah," Maggie said. "I know." David had been planning to do it. "Do you want a glass of wine?" she asked Wyatt.

"Sure," he said, and followed her inside, Coco on his heels.

They walked into the kitchen, and Maggie poured Wyatt a glass of wine at the small butcher block island, then led him back into the living room. She slowed by the couch, then passed it and sat down on the window seat that David had built when Sky was a toddler. Coco sat at her feet and watched Wyatt, who stopped and stood near the couch.

"Well. I see this is going to be bad," he said.

"Why?"

"We're not going to sit on the couch," he said. He took a good swallow of his wine. "How much wine do we have?

"Probably not enough," she said quietly.

Wyatt walked over to the coffee table across from her and sat down on it. He watched her take a big drink of her own.

"Tell me," he said.

Maggie looked up at him and swallowed hard. It took a moment for her to say it, and Wyatt watched her, frowning.

"I never should have been on the Gregory Boudreaux case," she finally said. "And I should have told you that at the scene when you asked me if I knew him."

"Okay," he said cautiously. "So you knew him."

"No."

Wyatt said nothing, just looked confused. Maggie blew out a breath. "He raped me when I was fifteen."

So many different emotions flashed in Wyatt's eyes at once that she couldn't identify even one, and she looked away from him, stared at a picture of Sky and Kyle instead. It was one thing to have Boudreaux looking at her, knowing, but Wyatt was something altogether different. She wasn't ashamed of having been attacked, she was just unaccustomed to it being known.

"What happened?" Wyatt asked quietly.

Maggie still couldn't bring herself to look at him. She changed her focus to a lamp instead. "I was fishing on the river. Back in the woods, not too far from here. I have no idea what he was doing there."

Wyatt stood up and Maggie turned away from the lamp and watched him walk to the window by the front door. His shoulders were bunched up, and when he reached a palm out to the window frame, he looked like he was going to slap it, then he just leaned on it, the other hand on his hip.

"You're angry," she said. She noticed that her fingers were hurting from holding her wine glass too tightly, and she set it down on the windowsill.

Wyatt shook his head, then ran a hand through his hair and turned around. "Of course I'm angry," he said.

"I know I messed up—"

"I haven't even gotten to that part yet," he said tightly.

"Then what are you angry about?"

"What do you mean—I'm angry because it's you," he snapped. "I'm angry because he hurt you! I'm angry—"

He put his hands on his hips and looked down at the floor for a second before looking at her again. "Because you're my best friend," he said quietly.

The honesty in his eyes as they looked at each other made her forget to breathe for a moment, and made her forget that there was a lot more to say.

"You're the only best friend I have left," she said softly.

"Well, then we're equally screwed," he said quietly. Maggie knew he was trying to lighten up a moment that wasn't going to get any lighter, but she appreciated his effort.

He walked back to the coffee table and sat down again. "Why didn't you just tell me?" he asked.

"Wyatt, I've never told anyone," she said. "I never even told David."

He looked down at her hands, then gently took hold of her wrists and rubbed them with his thumbs. Maggie blew out another breath.

"I'm sorry, but there's more that I need to tell you."

Wyatt looked up at her.

"Wilmette was there, too," she said.

"Oh crap, Maggie," he said, and he let go of her hands and covered his face. "Holy crap."

"Wyatt, I need you to understand, I didn't even know about it until after I had the case," she said.

He took his hands away from his face. "Explain that. Please."

"I have flashbacks sometimes. Sometimes I have dreams," she said.

"The old lady chasing you on the beach," he said.

"How do you know about that?"

"David. David told me."

Tears welled up in Maggie's eyes and she blinked them away.

"I know I've been keeping things from you. Important things," she said. "But in almost thirty years, that's the only thing I ever lied to David about. But he would have killed him. Do you understand?"

Wyatt nodded at the floor. "Yes. Yes, I do understand."

"There's no old lady," she said. "It was always just Gregory Boudreaux. But, after I started working his case, I remembered that there was someone else there. I never saw him. But Gregory said something to him. I never even remembered that until a few weeks ago."

Wyatt looked up at her. "If you never saw him, how'd you find out it was Wilmette?"

Maggie swallowed and chewed the corner of her lip. "Boudreaux told me," she said quietly.

Wyatt blinked at her a few times. "Boudreaux told you."

"Well, he told me without actually telling me," she said. "When I was interviewing him about Wilmette. I thought about telling you then. I think I was going to tell you. But then David…"

"Of course, Boudreaux," he said almost sarcastically.

Wyatt sighed and stood back up. He seemed to not know which direction to go in, then walked around the couch and leaned on the back of it.

"Why would Boudreaux tell you? Was it a slip, did he think you knew?"

"No. He just told me."

"Why?"

Maggie shrugged a little. "I'm not really sure."

"What the hell is it with you and Boudreaux, Maggie?"

"I think he likes me."

"Boudreaux doesn't like people. He collects people. Either he has something *on* them or he does something *for* them."

"Why are you mad at me?' Maggie snapped.

"I'm not mad at you!" he snapped back. "How can I be mad at you when you just told me you were raped?" He grabbed one of the couch pillows and slammed it back down. "That's not true. I am mad at you, but I'm mad because everything you've done or found regarding Wilmette is going to be suspect."

"I know." Maggie took a deep breath. "And Boudreaux killed Wilmette."

Wyatt stared at Maggie a moment, his face expressionless. "Why?"

"I thought it was because Wilmette wanted money. For staying quiet about it," Maggie said. "But I think it's because he disapproves of rape."

"Well. That's nice."

"He has a moral code, it's just a little different," Maggie said, and wondered why she felt the need to defend Boudreaux.

"Evidently," Wyatt said. "I assume, and I hope to hell it's true, that if you had some concrete evidence of this, we would have had this conversation already."

"I don't have anything concrete, no." Maggie took a swallow of her wine. "We already knew Wilmette went to Sea-Fair that Tuesday night. Boudreaux told us that. But I can't find anyone who saw him after that. And this processing room."

"What processing room?"

"It's new. Boudreaux expanded into fish. The processing room wasn't even in use yet when Wilmette went missing.

But it's a perfect place for chopping up a body before you dump it into the ocean."

Maggie tried not to dwell on the fact that she happened to like someone who she was pretty sure had chopped up a body. The killing didn't bother her so much; she had killed, too. But the chopping made her skin crawl.

"Wonderful," Wyatt said. He sighed and looked at Maggie. "You realize this isn't going to be a secret anymore. If I try to get a search warrant for Sea-Fair, I'm probably going to have to give a judge a better reason than the fact that no one saw Wilmette after that meeting."

"I know."

"And if we actually get to indict the guy, then motive comes into play. And the fact that you withheld information."

"I know," Maggie said again. "Just...let me tell my parents and the kids first if and when it comes to that."

Wyatt nodded and looked out the window behind her. "I'm pissed on a professional level, as your boss. I'm pissed on a personal level, too. I understand, intellectually, why you did what you did. But my feelings are hurt that you've kept so much from me so easily." He looked at her. "That scares me."

"It wasn't as easy as you probably think," she said quietly. There was a tickling in her chest, a fear that something that had barely started might end.

Wyatt opened his mouth to say something, but his cell phone interrupted. He pulled it out of his back pocket, saw the call was from Dwight, and put it on speaker.

"Hey, Dwight," he said.

"Hey, boss," Dwight said, sounding more flustered than usual. "We need you over on the island, real quick."

"What's going on?"

"We got some bodies washed up on the beach," Dwight said.

"Aw, crap. Which beach?"

"Uh, well...that's the thing, Wyatt," Dwight said. "It's all of 'em. All the beaches."

CHAPTER
FIVE

Maggie pulled in right behind Wyatt, parking in the sea grass off of Leisure Lane. Their location was an oceanfront piece of undeveloped land between two sections of vacation rentals. Short roads and driveways had been put in for about six rental houses, then construction had halted, for one reason or another. Those roads and driveways were now packed with police cruisers, Sheriff's Office cruisers, fire trucks, EMT vehicles, several Coast Guard vehicles, and a few dark sedans of indeterminate governmental origin.

Maggie grabbed her crime scene kit out of the back, then ran to catch up with Wyatt, who was halfway to the beach. Once they climbed to the top of the dunes, she realized with a heart-stopping certainty that she would not be using her kit at all.

The beach was covered in lights for several hundred yards in either direction. Lights from Coast Guard cutters just offshore. Spotlights on tripods scattered across the sand. Lights from emergency vehicles, flashlights, and the back decks of vacation rental homes, where people from

Ohio or Georgia stood at the rails and watched. Crossing in front of all the lights were the figures of Coast Guard and responders and Sheriff's deputies.

Some of them were attending to the two bodies already zipped into gray body bags. Others were bent over four more that were simply dark shapes on the sand where there should be none.

Neither Wyatt nor Maggie said a word. After a moment, Wyatt started down the dunes and Maggie followed. Dwight ran up to them as they walked down the sand toward the largest cluster of activity.

"Boss, I'm sorry," Dwight said, his eyes wide and his face strained. "We got so...so busy, and I forgot to call you for a little."

"What the hell happened, Dwight? Did a cruise ship sink out there?"

"We don't know what happened, Wyatt," Dwight said, as he fell in step with Wyatt and Maggie. "Coast Guard says there's been no distress signals or anything, but Lord have mercy."

He raised his arm and pointed at more lights behind them, just discernible some distance down the beach. "They've got at least three down there near Schooner Landing," he said, then stopped and turned and pointed the other way. "There's more down there, almost at the State Park."

Maggie and Wyatt looked at each other. Dwight swallowed hard, and his voice broke as he spoke. "And there's kids. Little kids. I hear there's at least a couple of kids, up by the State Park."

Maggie's heart lurched, and she wanted to pray, but she didn't know what to ask. That this would all be gone? That it would un-happen somehow?

"Did you know the Coast Guard is pretty much under Homeland Security?" Dwight asked. "I didn't know that."

"What's Homeland Security have to do with it?" Wyatt asked.

"Well, they're all Mexican, or Central American maybe."

"Ah, geez," Wyatt said, barely audible over the rain and the wind off the water. He started walking again.

Dwight struggled to keep up with Wyatt, whose legs were longer than most of Dwight's body. "There's four guys here from the actual Homeland Security, and they say it's their show, them and the Coast Guard."

"Which one of them is in charge?" Wyatt asked.

Dwight pointed to a man around fifty years old, with close-cropped gray hair, wearing khaki pants and a dark polo shirt. He was kneeling beside one of the bodies on the sand, tapping into a tablet. "That guy. Thompson or something like that."

The three of them walked over there, and Wyatt stopped next to the gray-haired man. "I'm Sheriff Hamilton," he said simply.

The man looked up, then stood and held out a hand. "Agent Tomlinson. Aaron."

"Wyatt," Wyatt said, and shook the man's hand. "This is Lt. Maggie Redmond."

Tomlinson and Maggie nodded at each other, then Tomlinson turned back to Wyatt. "We've got eleven so far. Nine on the beaches and two that the Coast Guard have pulled out of the water out there."

"Drowned?"

"That's what it looks like, but of course we don't know. We haven't found a boat. There was a hell of a storm out there earlier, though."

The rain was letting up, and Maggie pulled her wet hair out of her face, looked down at the body beside them. It was a man, definitely Hispanic, and she guessed Central American rather than Mexican. He looked to be in his late twenties.

He was wearing a silver chain with a Catholic medal on it, though she couldn't tell which one. Twisted around in the chain was a length of what looked like red yarn. Maggie glanced over at Tomlinson and Wyatt, but they were walking away.

Maggie knelt down and peered under one side of the open button-down shirt. There was a round pendant of some kind, maybe an ornament or a button. It looked handmade. Dwight bent over her as she lifted the fabric with one finger.

Maggie looked up as two Coast Guard headed toward them with a body bag. She stood up, blinking warm moisture from her eyes.

"What was it?" Dwight asked quietly.

"Minnie Mouse," Maggie said.

⚓   ⚓   ⚓

Several hours later, the total number of bodies had risen to fourteen. One more had been discovered down the beach, and two more pulled from the ocean by a Coast Guard cutter. The cutter had also located an inflatable dinghy with an outboard motor, built for a maximum of five or six passengers. They'd almost missed their chance to spot it; it had just barely enough air left in it to keep the outboard from pulling it under.

Maggie and Wyatt had been largely unwanted and unneeded, but also unwilling to leave, so they had helped when they could, but mainly been just another couple of witnesses to something no one there wanted to see.

They were standing by the dunes sharing a warm can of Coke that Dwight had scrounged up, when Tomlinson approached them, looking older than he had when they'd gotten there.

"Okay, the Coast Guard's running the dinghy and the bodies they've recovered to the marina. A couple of the ambulances will pick them up." He rubbed at his face and sighed. "Your medical examiner doesn't have enough room in his lab at the hospital, so some of the bodies will be taken to a funeral home downtown somewhere."

"Stephenson's," Wyatt said.

"Yeah. There isn't a single ID on any of these people, but we've got some plastic bags with pictures and letters and things; we'll see what we can do with those."

Wyatt offered the Coke to Maggie, but she shook her head. He drained the last of it. "Okay," he said. "We're going to head back to town. I realize this is your show, but as far as any kind of liaison between you and us, Maggie's your contact."

Maggie started to say something, then shut her mouth.

"Do me a favor and text me your number," Tomlinson said, handing her one of his cards.

"Okay," she said.

Tomlinson looked at Wyatt. "I do have some paperwork I need you to sign, Sheriff."

"Okay," Wyatt said.

Maggie called after him as he started off after Tomlinson. "I'm going to the car."

Wyatt held up a hand to acknowledge that and kept on walking. Maggie turned and headed back toward the lot where they'd parked.

There were a few oceanfront vacation rentals between her and the empty lots. All were dark. She was halfway past the last one, just on the edge of the undeveloped lots, when someone spoke to her.

"Did they find anyone living?"

Maggie started, and looked up to see Bennett Boudreaux leaning on the deck rail. The sky was just beginning to turn pink, but he held a rocks glass half-full of an amber liquid. He was wearing the same clothes she'd seen him in yesterday, and he looked like he hadn't slept.

"What are you doing here?" she asked.

"This is one of mine," he said. Maggie knew Boudreaux owned several vacation rentals on the island. It was one of many different streams of income. "Did they find anyone alive?"

Maggie sighed. "No."

Boudreaux nodded, drained half his glass and walked inside through the open sliding glass door. Maggie stood there for a moment, then climbed over the dune to the empty lots.

She was leaning on the hood of her Jeep when Wyatt arrived. She couldn't remember the last time she'd seen him look so exhausted.

"I don't want this, Wyatt," she said.

"Nobody wants it, Maggie," he said, fishing his keys out of his jeans pocket. "But the fact is, I don't have any other open cases I can give you. Unless you want to take vacation or start working patrol, this is what I've got."

They looked at each other a moment, then Maggie nodded.

"You know, my Dad always said you can tell a lot about people by what washes up on the beaches," Wyatt said. "He was talking about hypodermics and beer bottles, but I wonder what this says."

Maggie watched Wyatt as he looked back toward the beach.

"Let's get out of here," Wyatt said, and opened his door.

⚓   ⚓   ⚓

Wyatt drove along Gulf Beach Drive, headed for 300, also known as the bridge, which would take him to Eastpoint, where he and Maggie would pick up the other bridge back to Apalach. The only other vehicle on the road was one of the EMT trucks, several blocks ahead. Maggie's was the only vehicle on the road behind him.

There wasn't much to Gulf Beach Drive, or to Saint George Island, which was only half a mile wide in most places. Bayside vacation rentals lined the left side of the road, oceanfront houses lined the right. There were only a couple of places to eat or pick up groceries, get gas or hit an ATM.

A few blocks shy of the turn to the bridge, Wyatt passed a little pizza place on the corner. It was as nondescript as such a place could be, with a gravel parking lot and a few benches and tables on a small deck.

As he passed, Wyatt noticed a kid or teenager with dark brown hair sitting at one of the tables. Wyatt looked away to grab a half empty Mountain Dew from the console and unscrewed it, then put it back down and turned on his left turn signal before making a U-turn without slowing. There had been no cars in the gravel lot at the pizza place.

Wyatt passed Maggie, who had slowed down and was frowning at him as he passed. He pulled into the gravel lot and got out of the car. He could hear Maggie turning behind him.

As Wyatt walked up the ramp to the deck, he saw that the kid was a boy, maybe eight or nine years old. He was wearing cut offs, and a Pokémon tee shirt under an open gray hoodie. He watched, expressionless, as Wyatt approached.

"Hi," Wyatt said. The kid looked at him warily, but said nothing. "¡Hola!" Wyatt tried again. He could hear Maggie parking in the gravel behind him and he wanted her to hurry up. His Spanish sucked; hers was slightly better.

"Habla Ingles?" The boy shook his head, but just barely. "Está bien. Soy amigo."

The boy didn't seem to think Wyatt looked like much of a friend. Wyatt sighed with relief when Maggie stopped beside him.

"What's going—oh." Maggie looked at the boy, who seemed twice as alarmed with twice as many strangers standing there.

"Ask him his name," Wyatt said. "Where his parents are."

"Me llamo Maggie," Maggie said. "¿Cómo te llamas?"

The boy looked from Maggie to Wyatt, then back at Maggie.

"Virgilio," he said, barely above a whisper.

"Virgilio," Maggie repeated. "¿Dónde está su familia?"

The little boy looked at her for a long moment, then stretched out his arm and pointed toward the beach.

"Dammit," Wyatt whispered.

⚓　⚓　⚓

Wyatt thought it best for Virgilio to ride with Maggie, so he followed them to the docks, where Tomlinson was handling the transfer of the bodies from the Coast Guard cutter. Maggie scrounged up a bottle of water from her console, and her heart broke a little when the child downed it all at once.

She tried to engage him a few times on the fifteen-minute drive, unsuccessfully, and finally just let him sit in the back seat without being accosted by questions.

The sun still wasn't all the way up, but when they pulled up to the marina, pockets of locals stood nearby, silently watching as the gray body bags were unloaded from cutter to truck. Maggie turned off the Jeep and sat, unsure about exposing Virgilio to the scene, wondering which of the gray bags might hold one of his parents.

Wyatt walked up to her window and tapped, and Maggie rolled it partway down.

"Wait here a minute," he said, and walked off toward the group of Coast Guard and deputies and Homeland Security guys.

Maggie watched him as he located Tomlinson in the crowd and pulled him aside. Tomlinson looked over at Maggie's Jeep, and she had a momentary urge to drive away with Virgilio, to take him home and lock her doors.

Wyatt and Tomlinson spoke for a moment, then they walked over to the Jeep. Maggie tamped down her fight-or-flight response and rolled down her window.

Tomlinson looked into the back seat and sighed, then looked at Maggie.

"Have you gotten anything else out of him?" he asked quietly.

"No."

Tomlinson leaned one hand on her window frame and spoke to Virgilio softly, in perfect Spanish. The boy didn't answer. When Maggie glanced in her rear view mirror to look at him, he was looking back at her.

"Está bien, mijo," she said.

"Virgilio," Tomlinson said. "¿De dónde eres?" *Where are you from?*

Maggie watched the boy in the mirror as he took a moment to answer. She didn't understand his first reply, but when Tomlinson asked another question, he answered, "Guatemala."

Tomlinson asked the boy who was with him, and the answer was given so softly that Maggie barely heard it. "Mi mamá. Mi papá. Mi hermana pequeña." *My mom, my dad, my little sister.*

Maggie blinked a few times as her eyes filled, and she tried to cover it by opening her door. Tomlinson and Wyatt stepped back as she quickly got out.

"You're not going to ask him to identify them, are you?" she whispered, forgetting that the boy didn't understand English.

"We might have to, if we can't do it ourselves," Tomlinson answered. He was quiet, but he didn't bother whispering. "But don't worry, I'm not a robot. I've got three boys of my own."

"What are we going to do with him?" Wyatt asked.

"I'll need him to stay with us," Tomlinson said. "We're gonna stay at the Bayview for a couple of days at least, instead of driving back and forth to Tallahassee."

"He doesn't have anything. He doesn't even have something to change into," Maggie said. "Can I bring him some of my son's things?"

"Yeah, that's fine. I'd appreciate that," Tomlinson said. He looked back through the front window. "Virgilio," he said. "Ven conmigo, okay?" *Come with me.*

"Do you have to take him now?" Maggie asked.

"I need to talk to him while everything, anything, is fresh in his mind, Lieutenant."

"He's scared," Maggie answered. "And he's probably exhausted and hungry."

"I understand. I'll make sure he's okay, but he needs to come with me now."

Maggie looked at Virgilio through the back window. He looked even smaller than he already had, and his eyes were wide as he listened to their conversation. She sighed and opened the back door.

"Está bien, Virgilio," she said for what seemed like the tenth time. She rummaged through her brain for the right words. "Él va a cuidar de ti." *He'll take care of you.*

She held out her hand, and after a moment, the little boy climbed out of the Jeep, though he didn't take her hand. Tomlinson gently put a hand on the child's shoulder.

"You're not taking him over there, are you?" Wyatt asked.

"No, I'll have someone walk him over to the hotel." The Bayview was right on the marina, just half a block away.

"Okay," Maggie said, as though her agreement was needed.

Maggie and Wyatt watched Tomlinson walk the boy over to another agent, a woman, who was writing on a pad near one of the dark sedans.

Maggie watched the two agents talk for a moment, as the little boy stood there between them, a bystander to his own immediate future. Then her attention was caught by the sight of William and Robert, the florists, as they stood on the sidewalk, watching the activity.

They looked decidedly sad, and Maggie's respect for them went up several notches. She was certain that their expressions had nothing to do with a threat to their business.

Her attention was drawn away from the crowd at the docks when Wyatt opened her door.

"Go home and get some sleep," he said.

Maggie opened her mouth to say something vaguely nurturing, then changed her mind and got in. Wyatt put both hands on her window frame and closed her door, leaning for a moment.

"Wyatt?"

He looked at her for a moment, and she tried to read the emotions beneath the exhaustion.

"Neither one of us is up to talking about it right now, Maggie," he said. "It's really not something we should be trying to think about when our asses are dragging and our hearts are broken. It'll keep."

Maggie looked up at him, trying to gauge whether he was distancing himself from her or just worn out.

"It'll keep," he said again, quietly. Then he turned and headed for his car.

Maggie watched him walk away, and she felt an additional weight of sadness settle into her chest, and just a little bit of fear.

She picked her cell phone up off the passenger seat and speed-dialed her parents. It was only seven, but the only time her Dad had slept past five-thirty was a couple of years ago, when he was recovering from having part of his left lung removed. Now, he only went out on the oyster beds a few days a week, but he was still up before the sun.

Gray Redmond answered on the second ring. "Hey, Sunshine," he said, his voice at once soft and gravelly.

"Hey, Daddy," Maggie said. "Are you working?"

"No, I'm home this morning."

"Are the kids up yet?"

"I'm sure Sky will be up at the crack of dinner, but Kyle's up," her father answered. "We're going to do some fishing out back. Are you at the marina?"

"Yeah."

"You been there all night?"

"Yes."

"It's a horrible thing."

"Yes," she said again. "Can I come over and have some coffee?"

"Door's unlocked, Sunshine."

CHAPTER

SIX

Maggie's parents lived on a stretch of Hwy 98, just a couple of miles outside town, right on the bay. They'd bought it back when such property was both available and affordable. Though that part of the road was a mixture of older, modest houses and fishing related businesses, the property today would have been way out of her parents' reach. Her mother had been a homemaker her entire adult life, her father an oysterman.

Maggie drove down the gravel drive that ran through the deep, narrow lot, and parked in front of the pale yellow house where she had been raised. She found her parents in the kitchen at the back of the house.

"Morning, you guys," she said.

"Morning, baby," he Dad said.

"Oh, honey, you look wrecked," Georgia Redmond said, and got up from the table.

Georgia was one of those women who was strikingly beautiful without doing a single thing to enhance her beauty. With thick, dark brown hair that curled around her shoulders, large green eyes, and a tiny waist, she still

turned men's heads at fifty-eight, even though she genuinely never noticed. She had been madly in love with tall,
skinny, soft-spoken Gray since high school.

Maggie accepted a hug from her mother, breathing in
the comforting scents of gardenia, cotton and coconut oil,
then Georgia pulled out a chair.

"Sit down honey, and I'll get you some coffee," Georgia
said. "Are you hungry?"

"No, thanks, Mom." Maggie sat down heavily in the
yellow-flowered chair that she'd occupied for nearly every
meal of her youth.

"We heard what happened on the radio," Gray said.
"What's going on down there?"

Maggie sighed. "We found a little boy. Alive. He's the
only one."

"Oh, bless his heart," Georgia said, setting Maggie's cup
down in front of her.

"Yeah. I wanted to ask Kyle if it was okay for me to take
him some of his old clothes, maybe a toy or something."

"He's just in the bathroom," Georgia said. "What's going to happen to the boy?"

Maggie shrugged and shook her head. "I have no idea.
Homeland Security is in charge of everything. I would
imagine they'll get him home, sooner or later."

"What about his family?" Gray asked. "Were they out
there, too?"

"He lost his parents and his little sister."

They sat in silence for a moment, while Maggie stirred
milk and sugar into her coffee.

"Hey, Mom."

Maggie looked up and smiled as Kyle walked in. He
was ten years old, but looked much younger. He had David's slight build, glossy black hair, and long, thick lashes.

When she looked at him these days, her heart couldn't decide whether to wither or bloom.

"Hey, baby," she said, as he gave her neck a quick hug. "I hear you and Granddad are going fishing."

"Yeah, we're gonna catch something for lunch," Kyle said, as he grabbed some toast and bacon from a plate on the counter. "Granddad says I have to do one thing outside before I can play Minecraft."

"We figured you'd been up all night, Maggie," Georgia said. "So we thought we'd just keep them here for the day, let you get some rest."

Maggie nodded and watched Kyle, her safe, privileged child, sit down at the other end of the table.

"That's really sad about those people," he said. "Did they have an accident?"

"We don't know yet," Maggie answered. "There was a little boy who survived. He's a little younger than you. He doesn't have anything, nothing at all. Do you mind if I give him some things of yours, maybe some things you don't want anymore?"

Kyle thought a moment, staring into the air. "You think he likes Marvel comics?"

"I don't know. He can't read English."

Kyle shrugged. "He can look at the pictures. Take him some."

"Okay. I'm going to take him some of your old clothes that I keep meaning to take to the church," she said.

Kyle munched on a piece of bacon. "You should take him some Transformers. Take him Bumblebee, he's everybody's favorite."

"I thought you were keeping them as a collection," Maggie said.

Kyle shrugged. "They're just sitting there. Take him Starscream, too, so he has a bad guy."

"Which one is Starscream?"

"Geez, Mom," Kyle said. He softened his eye roll with a grin. "Just take him some big silver guys."

Maggie tried to smile back, but she felt like someone had scraped her soul with sandpaper. She took a drink of her coffee and tried not to look as bad as she felt.

Kyle wrapped his bacon up in his toast and stood. "Ready, Granddad?"

"Keep your shirt on, I'm coming," Gray answered as he stood and stretched. He kissed the top of Maggie's head. "Go get some sleep, Sunshine."

"I will, Daddy."

Gray and Kyle went out the sliding door onto the back deck, and Maggie watched them grab poles, the tackle box, and a bucket, and head through the back yard to the bay.

"Honey, you want to just stay here and lie down in the guest room?" Georgia asked, frowning.

Maggie looked at her mother and sighed. "I can't. I need to take care of Coco and the chickens. And take this little boy some stuff."

"Do you promise you'll go home and go to bed afterwards?"

"Yeah, I will."

"You look so sad."

Maggie gave her mother half a smile, then looked down into her coffee. "Mom, you remember when you told me that you and Daddy almost didn't get married, but you got a second chance?"

Georgia blinked a couple of times, then took a sip of her coffee. "Sure."

"I think I might have blown it with Wyatt," Maggie said softly.

Georgia put her coffee mug down. "With Wyatt? Aw, no, sweetie, I doubt that. Why?"

"I kept something from him. Something important, but please don't ask me what."

"And now you've told him?"

Maggie nodded, and Georgia ran a finger around the edge of her cup. "Well, I've found that it's a lot easier for a man to recover from the truth than it is for him to feel lied to. Wyatt's a strong man, Maggie. Whatever it is, just give him some time."

"I'm afraid that I killed something before it really got started, Mom."

Georgia looked at Maggie for a moment. "Honey, I just don't think Wyatt scares that easily. You're probably still going to have to deal with falling in love with him."

Maggie gave a nervous laugh. "Mom, I'm not in love with him."

Georgia put a hand on top of her daughter's. "You will be," she said simply.

⚓ ⚓ ⚓

Maggie got out of the Jeep, and could hear Coco going insane inside. The poor dog had been in all night, and Maggie hoped there weren't any surprises waiting for her. As she headed for the stairs, Stoopid, delighted that Coco wasn't available to impede his progress, pell-melled over from behind a hibiscus.

Maggie raised a hand to the rooster. "I already heard," she said, and he seemed to deflate a little He stumbled to a stop a few feet away, let her have one of his unimpressive crows, then ruffled his neck feathers and headed over to the chicken yard.

Once inside, Maggie rubbed away Coco's impending cardiac arrest, apologized several times, then let the dog out and headed for Kyle's room. She stopped by the foot of Kyle's bed and looked around her, really looking for the first time in a while.

They had never had a lot. David had worked like a dog as a shrimper, and she had worked her way up in the Sheriff's Office, but they'd never made more than they'd needed. Vacations were cheap and close by, sneakers were serviceable rather than celebrity-endorsed, and the kids worked hard to earn their modest allowances.

But Kyle had so much, when Maggie looked at his situation through the lens of the last several hours. His Xbox had been a Christmas gift from her parents, but he had one. There were three shelves of books, and more action figures, board games, and videos than she could count. She wasn't sure what was there, but she knew there was food in the fridge. Kyle had gone through tragedy, but he had never been hungry and he had never been alone.

Maggie pulled Kyle's backpack from last year out of his closet, and put in the Bumblebee action figure and a couple of big silver guys she hoped were villains. She added some comic books from the bottom of Kyle's stack, then rummaged through his desk drawer and gathered a pack of markers and a pad of paper. On her way out of the room, she grabbed an unopened pack of underwear that she'd bought on sale for the coming school year. She wasn't sure they'd fit, but they were better than nothing.

After putting together a few changes of clothes that Kyle had outgrown, and feeding the chickens and Coco, Maggie wandered around the house, finding a few other odd things to take to the little boy, then she climbed back into the Jeep, blinked her scratchy eyes a few times against the full morning sun, and headed back into town.

⚓ ⚓ ⚓

The Homeland Security team had opted to stay at the Bay-view hotel rather than run back and forth to Tallahassee. The hotel was a two-story brick building right on Scipio Creek, the channel of the Apalachicola River that eventually opened into the bay. The rooms were accessed by an outdoor hallway right over the marina, and Maggie kept her eyes averted from it as she knocked on the door to room 212. David's shrimp boat had been blown up just a short way down the creek, and Maggie had yet to be able to look at it without feeling like someone was scooping out her insides with a spoon.

The female agent from earlier opened the door. She was about Maggie's height, but only in her late twenties, with an efficiently short cut to her blond hair and no sign of makeup.

"Lieutenant Redmond?" she asked quietly.

"Yes."

"He's sleeping, but come on in," the agent said, stepping back.

Maggie stepped inside, Kyle's Star Wars backpack in one hand, two grocery bags of clothes in the other.

The agent closed the door quietly. "I'm Gerri Winters."

Maggie nodded at her and looked toward the back of the room. The front of the room held a small sitting area and a kitchenette. Beyond it, separated by a curtain that had been left open, was a sleeping area with two full-sized beds. There was a very small lump in one of them.

"I brought him some clothes and things, a few toys," Maggie said softly. "I wasn't sure what you'd have time to grab for him, so there's a toothbrush and a pack of toothpaste in here, too."

"Thanks. One of us was going to run out later, but this is helpful."

"How's he doing?"

The agent shrugged. "We talked to him for a little bit, then just let him go to bed. He was asleep before he put his head down."

Maggie nodded. "Should I just put these things in there?"

Gerri nodded. "Yeah, just put them on top of the dresser."

Maggie walked back to the sleeping area, gently set the grocery bags on top of a cheap oak dresser next to the bed where Virgilio was sleeping, then propped the backpack on the floor next to it.

She stood there and watched him for a minute, though she couldn't see anything but a shock of dark hair peeking out from under the covers. He was curled into a comma, his back to her. She could see the steady movement of his back as he breathed.

She reached into the side pocket of the backpack, pulled out a small, stuffed Mickey Mouse, and tucked it near his head on the pillow. Then she turned around and walked away.

CHAPTER
SEVEN

T he next morning, Maggie was sitting at her desk, filling out her report on the previous night, when Wyatt set a to-go cup from Cafe con Leche on her desk.

"Gertrudis says hi," he said.

Maggie looked up at Wyatt with pure gratitude. He had his own cup of coffee in hand. "Oh, my gosh, thank you," she said.

"They miss you over there."

Maggie took a long swallow of her *café con leche* and sighed. "I miss them, too."

"She also said that if you need to, you can call ahead from your car and she'd run your coffee around the corner to you," Wyatt said.

"I'd feel stupid and melodramatic," Maggie said. "I can look at a river. I'll stop in there tomorrow morning."

Wyatt looked at his watch. "Tomlinson's on his way over to brief us on what he's got so far."

"Okay."

"What are you working on?"

Maggie shrugged. "I'm doing my prelim on last night. Hopefully, Tomlinson's got something I can do. Otherwise, I'm going to be waiting around for someone to rob the Piggly Wiggly."

"Well, I wouldn't count on getting much from Tomlinson," Wyatt said. "Nice guy, I like him. But he's going to include us only as much as he needs to."

Maggie sighed. "I'm sure that's true."

"Don't worry," Wyatt said as he headed out of her office. "Somebody's bound to kill somebody soon."

"You're always such a glass-half-full kinda guy," Maggie said to his back.

⚓   ⚓   ⚓

Half an hour later, Maggie rapped on the side of Wyatt's door and walked in. Tomlinson was leaning on Wyatt's desk drinking a cup of the office coffee. Wyatt was still drinking his, leaning back in his leather chair.

"Morning, Lieutenant," Tomlinson said.

"Agent Tomlinson," she answered, and sat down in one of the vinyl chairs in front of Wyatt's desk.

"Thank you for bringing that stuff by for the boy," Tomlinson said.

"How is he?" she asked.

"Sleeping, mostly. They were out there for at least three days. The kid's not real sure of the timeline."

Tomlinson sat down in the other vinyl chair and pulled out his tablet, tapped at it as he spoke. "His name is Virgilio Munoz. His father was Emilio, his mother Fernandina. His little sister, age four, was Lupe." He took a sip of his coffee and tapped at the screen again. "They're from a village about two hours inland from Amatique Bay, called

El Paraiso. I've been to that area, and I'm here to tell you there's nothing about it that'll remind you of paradise."

He drained his coffee and set the empty cup on the desk.

"He's not absolutely positive how many people were traveling. Coast Guard hasn't recovered any more bodies, though. He really only paid attention to his own family and the other kids on board. There were two, besides him and his sister."

"Did he tell you what the hell happened?" Wyatt asked.

"Yeah, pretty much. From his limited perspective," Tomlinson said. "From what I can put together, there was an argument between Virgilio's dad, a couple of other passengers and the guys that were running the boat. Americans, by the way. They were supposed to get the passengers closer to shore, but they decided to put them out sooner."

"Does Virgilio know why?" Maggie asked.

"No. Could have been the weather, could have been a fuel issue, maybe they saw another vessel that made them nervous. Who knows?" Tomlinson said. "To make matters worse, there were originally two dinghies, but they had a problem with the outboard on the other one, and piled everybody into one. That dinghy wasn't meant to hold more than five people. According to the Coast Guard, the four-stroke they had mounted on it was way too heavy, too, and too light in horsepower."

"Do you have any idea yet who these Americans were that were running them here?" Wyatt asked.

"Not yet. The boy says the word 'wave' was in the boat name, which is probably going to give us a ton of hits. He has no idea what kind of boat it was. His people were farmers. But, the boat was out of Texas, he could read that," Tomlinson answered.

"Lot of boats in Texas," Wyatt said, sighing.

"No kidding," Tomlinson said. "So, according to what the kid told me, they got into some pretty big swells out there. The storm had already broken when they were put in the dinghy. They were already taking on water because of the weight, but he thinks they got a hole in the stern, because it pretty much went under, and the outboard conked. I'm waiting to hear from the Guard on that. Anyway, everybody ended up in the water."

"Where were they going?" Wyatt asked.

"Here," Tomlinson said. "They were coming here."

"What for?" Maggie asked. "I mean, what were they going to do when they got here?"

"They had work lined up. Picking vegetables on a farm not far from here. According to Virgilio, they were going to work for some rich man with a big farm."

Maggie's stomach felt like someone had just reached into it. She put her elbow on the arm of the chair and put her face in her hand.

"What?" Wyatt asked.

Maggie looked up at him. "Boudreaux."

"Boudreaux what?" Wyatt asked.

Tomlinson looked from Maggie to Wyatt and back again.

"He was at the beach last night. On the deck of one his vacation rentals."

"Who's Boudreaux?"

"Local rich guy. Dabbles in a lot of things," Wyatt said. "Also figures in two other cases I have on my hands."

"Two?" Tomlinson asked.

"Well, we don't have a wide selection of criminals in Apalach," Wyatt said. "We try to make the most of what we've got."

"So what about him?" Tomlinson asked Maggie.

"He has a couple of farms. A melon farm over near Live Oak. I don't know where the other one is."

"So what makes you think he has anything to do with this?"

"I've never seen Boudreaux look anything less than perfect. He doesn't dress up much, but even dressed down, he's immaculate," Maggie said. "But he was wearing the same clothes I'd seen him in earlier that day. He was all wrinkled. And he was drinking scotch at sunrise."

Maggie realized that Wyatt might think she'd intentionally withheld this information and she jerked her head his way. "I thought he must have had a fight with his wife or something."

Tomlinson looked at Wyatt. "What do you think?"

"Nothing would surprise me where Boudreaux's concerned," Wyatt said, sounding tired.

"Where do I find him?"

"He's got a business called Sea-Fair about a block north of the Bayview," Wyatt said. Maggie wished he would look at her.

"Okay, I'll look in on him. I really don't have anything, so I don't expect him to offer anything, but maybe I can get a feel for the guy."

"Can I go with you?" Maggie asked. She wanted to see Boudreaux's face when Tomlinson questioned him, wanted to see for herself whether he seemed to be telling the truth, regardless of what he actually said.

"I'm sorry, but I think I'll say no," Tomlinson said, not unkindly. "I will brief you guys once I've talked with him, though."

He sighed and scratched at his closely-cropped hair. "Damn sad shame. The boy's father pushed him and his sister up on top of the bow of the dinghy, which was still partly above water, and told him to hang on. Then he disappeared. A few other people managed to grab hold, too, but not for very long."

He rubbed at his face. "The dinghy was mostly underwater. At some point, the boy lost his grip on his little sister and let go of the dinghy to go after her, but he lost her. He woke up on the beach."

The three of them were silent for a moment. Maggie blinked a few times, then focused on the back of Wyatt's monitor to get a grip on her feelings. When she looked up at Wyatt, he was staring at his desk, his jaw clenched.

Tomlinson got up from his chair. "I'm gonna head over to this guy Boudreaux's. I'll get with you guys later on."

After he left, Wyatt and Maggie sat without speaking. The tapping of Wyatt's pencil on the edge of his desk was the only thing that broke the silence.

Maggie got up and walked out.

She walked down the hall to the ladies' room and opened the door, smiled at Deputy Sue Thornton, who was on her way out. She was relieved that no one else was in the bathroom.

She turned on one of the faucets and splashed cold water on her face. She felt her chest filling up, expanding, like someone was blowing up a balloon inside her. She yanked a couple of coarse brown paper towels out of the dispenser and held them under the water for a moment, then shut it off and walked into the stall furthest from the door.

She slapped the door shut and locked it, then covered her mouth and nose with the bunched up wet towels. Then she cried surprisingly hard, given the silence with which she did it.

EIGHT

Maggie was adrift.

She had no case to actually work. It was only three in the afternoon, and she had nowhere to be. She had thought about picking up the kids and taking them to the pool at the community center, but when she'd called her parents' house, she'd been advised by Georgia that they'd gone out on the oyster beds with Gray.

She found herself with nothing to do but think, and too many things she didn't want to think about. When she got off the bridge from Eastpoint into Apalach, she turned right, intending to go home, but the thought suddenly made her feel more alone than she wanted to be. Instead, she decided to stop at Boss Oyster. She hadn't eaten since the day before, and Gray would be coming in soon; she'd be able to see him and the kids as they passed Boss on the way to the marina.

She got a seat out on the deck, overlooking the docks and Scipio Creek. There were several other occupied tables, a mixture of tourists and locals, despite the almost malevolent heat. There was at least a slight breeze off of the water, and Maggie lifted her hair off her neck and tried to feel it as she sipped her sweet tea. She found herself wishing it was a glass of wine, or even a mojito, but she knew that she was feeling far too introspective for alcohol to be a good idea.

Something had been slowly unraveling inside her since she'd walked across the dunes and looked at Gregory Boudreaux's body lying on the beach. It was as though the string holding a package together was steadily working itself loose, and when it had finished, she would find that nothing was held together as neatly as before, that she would find that *she* was not as neatly put together as she had thought.

It had started with not telling Wyatt about her connection to Gregory. At that point, she had strayed from the very narrow path between right and wrong, law and unlawfulness that she had defined for herself.

Then Boudreaux had stepped into her life, and suddenly it was as though she were occupying two worlds. She was, in some ways, more honest with Boudreaux than she was with anyone else, and yet she was keeping secrets from Wyatt. She was even keeping Boudreaux's secrets, which had inexplicably become far too intertwined with her own.

For weeks now, she had been wondering who and what she actually was, with one foot on either side of a line that was becoming harder to see. She was almost grateful for the news that Boudreaux had probably been behind the deaths, or at least responsible for the deaths, of those poor Guatemalans. While it angered her, disappointed her, and even hurt her on some level she didn't want to define, it also made things easier. She didn't need to worry anymore about liking him a little too much for her own conscience.

She let out a breath and took another drink of her tea as she watched an egret float down and settle in the grass beneath one of the live oaks near the deck. The moment was ruined for her by the tourist in a Tommy Bahama shirt at the table to her right, who sat with his back to her, noisily sucking the meat from a Blue crab claw while his portly wife poked at a brochure with her oyster fork.

Apalach depended on the tourists, but there were days when she would have been happy to hear they'd stopped coming. She listened to the woman suggesting various plans for their stay, then tuned her out, annoyed with both her nasally voice and her apparently carefree week.

"Hello, Maggie."

Maggie started as she looked up at Boudreaux, standing there in a crisp blue linen shirt, a fresh bottle of Red Stripe beer in his hand. It was as though she'd conjured him up by thinking about him too hard.

"Mr. Boudreaux," she said automatically.

"I saw you out here when I walked in," he said. "Do you mind if I sit down?"

Maggie's first instinct was to say that she damn well did, but she thought better of it. Why shouldn't he sit down and be made to account for himself?

So she nodded, and he pulled out the chair on her right. The table next to them was quite close, and the man in the Tommy Bahama shirt glanced over his shoulder, a tidbit of crab meat on his lower lip, as Boudreaux's chair tapped his.

"Pardon me," Boudreaux said politely, and scooted his chair in as he sat.

Maggie looked out over the deck rail at the water, trying to corral all of the things she wanted to say into one cohesive mass.

"I've just been speaking to Agent Tomlinson," Boudreaux said quietly. "I needed some fresh air."

Maggie looked at him. His startling blue eyes were as sharp as ever, but there seemed to be a few more fine lines at their corners, a few more shadows beneath them.

"And how did that go?' she asked him.

"About like you'd expect," he answered. "Was it you that told him he should take a look at me?"

"Yes," she answered flatly.

"Well, there's nothing illogical in that, is there?" he asked mildly.

His eyes narrowed just a bit and cut over his shoulder for a split second, as the man in the Tommy Bahama shirt noisily sucked out some more crab meat. The wife was talking about going to the beach on the island.

"No, there isn't," Maggie said.

"You're upset with me," Boudreaux said.

"I'm a lot of things," she answered quietly. She felt the anger pressing against her throat from the inside.

Boudreaux opened his mouth to say something, then stopped as the crab man spoke up next to him.

"No, I don't want to go the beach," he was saying petulantly. "Not with all those bodies they found out there."

Boudreaux and Maggie stared at each other.

"Well, it's not like they're still there," the wife said.

"Whatever," the man said, then lowered his voice just a hair and spoke in a grumbling tone. "It's too bad and all, but I'm fed up with them coming here anyway, so they can live ten to a trailer and take American jobs."

Maggie stared back at Boudreaux. His left eye twitched almost imperceptibly, and he took a swallow of his beer and set it down gently before turning around in his chair and leaning close to the man.

"Do you know why they live ten to a trailer?' he asked quietly. "Because they all work two jobs, jobs no Americans want by the way, so they don't mind sharing bedrooms and eating ramen six days a week, because that means they can send more money home to the three generations of family they support."

Boudreaux's voice was quiet and level, but Maggie had never heard it sound quite so icy. She glanced around, but only one other person was paying attention, a local fisherman at the table across from them, who had stopped chewing his grouper sandwich and was watching Boudreaux.

"What the hell?" the crab man asked, surprised.

"You think you're superior to them because you're an American?" Boudreaux asked, somehow sounding almost polite. "Look at you. I can't see you doing manual labor sixteen hours a day so your kids can go to the doctor and your wife has something to feed them besides corn meal."

"Listen, friend—" the man started.

"No, you listen," Boudreaux said calmly. "And I'm not your friend, you arrogant redneck. You need to limit your conversation to things you understand, which I suspect is very little."

He stood up, without urgency, and Maggie's right hand automatically touched the Glock 23 in her back holster, though she didn't actually think she'd need it.

"You got a lotta nerve, buddy," the crab man said, but he looked less brave than he was trying to sound.

Boudreaux put a hand on the man's shoulder and bent down.

"I have more nerve than you should be comfortable with," he said quietly. "It's only out of respect for your wife that I don't put that crab claw through your right eye." He looked at the wife, who sat with her mouth open. "Please pardon the intrusion," Boudreaux said, "And enjoy the rest of your stay."

He turned and nodded at Maggie. "Maggie," he said, then quickly walked away. Maggie heard the screen door slap shut, and watched the crab man gather his wits.

"Who the hell does he think he is?" he asked weakly. The fisherman across the way let out a short, sharp laugh and both Maggie and the crab man looked at him.

"Dude, if you *knew* who he was you'd have crapped your pants. I almost did, and he wasn't even talking to me."

He went back to his grouper sandwich, and Maggie jumped up and went after Boudreaux.

⚓ ⚓ ⚓

By the time Maggie had hurried out to the parking lot, Boudreaux was almost back to Sea-Fair, just a few doors down. He was walking quickly and with a tightness to his gait that was unusual for him. Maggie ran to catch up, and he glanced over at her as she came abreast of him. His eyes were cold and hard, and he didn't slow his pace as they entered the oyster shell parking lot of his company.

"What was that about?" Maggie snapped.

"What do you think it was about?" he snapped back. "The man was a moron."

"You can't just go around threatening to poke crab claws through people's eyeballs," Maggie said.

"Why not? Because it will hurt my reputation, or because I was sitting with someone from the Sheriff's Office?"

"Because it's illegal," she shot back.

He cut his eyes at her. "That's probably the silliest thing you've ever said to me."

They reached his black Mercedes, and he stalked to the driver's side and opened his door. Maggie glared at him over the roof.

"I didn't say it to be cute," she snapped.

"And I didn't put his eye out," Boudreaux snapped back. Maggie had never actually seen him angry, and if she weren't so angry with him, it might have scared her a little. "I didn't have to, and you and I both know I have more self-control than that."

"I don't know as much as I thought," she said.

"What's that intended to mean?"

"Those people are dead! Children are dead!"

Boudreaux slammed a hand down on the roof of his car, and Maggie jerked back just a little. "I know good and damn well they're dead!" he said, raising his voice for the first time in her hearing. "The only person who's more aware of that than me is that little boy they've got over at the hotel!"

Maggie's eyes narrowed at the reminder.

Boudreaux took a deep breath. "Maggie, I'll be frank. I'm a little disappointed in you right now."

Maggie's mouth opened a couple of times before she could speak. "You're *disappointed* in me? What the hell for?"

"Because I might be a killer, but I'm not a degenerate," he said, without a trace of irony.

Maggie glared at him, pinching her lips shut to keep from screaming at him. He looked away, toward the front door of Sea-Fair, and Maggie saw him take a deep breath before he looked back at her.

"Get in the car," his voice smooth and quiet again.

"What?" Maggie asked incredulously.

"I'd like you to get in the car, please."

"Why?"

He stared at her a moment over the roof of the car. "Do you remember one time I told you that there might come a day when you might need to understand me just a little?"

Maggie did recall. She had asked him why they were suddenly having frequent and sometimes personal conversations, after decades of existing in the same town without ever having one.

"What about it?" she asked.

"This is one of those days," he said. "I want to show you something."

"Do you think I'm an idiot?" she asked him.

"No, I think you're just smart enough to get in your own way," he snapped. He reached into one his front pants pockets. "You have a 45-caliber pistol in your belt and probably another one in your purse or on your ankle. I have a pocket knife, which you may have."

He slid a long, thin knife across the roof, and she caught it as it started to fall. She'd seen him cut mangos with this knife and it had a wicked blade. She had no idea what else he might have done with it, but she couldn't help wondering if this was the knife he'd used to kill Wilmette.

"Please come with me," Boudreaux said, making an effort to keep his voice even.

Maggie stared at him a moment, and he slapped the roof again, though not as hard as before.

"Get in the car, dammit."

Maggie knew who and what he was. She knew what he had done. Yet, she'd never felt afraid in his presence; in fact, she had sometimes been oddly comforted by it. But she'd never seen him display anger before, and she couldn't help the tingling in her stomach.

She's always known that he wanted something from her, that he wasn't just befriending her out of guilt or curiosity. She was also a police officer, and he was a killer who knew she knew that. It would be stupid to get into his car.

She opened the door and got in anyway.

She settled onto the soft beige leather of the passenger seat and shut her door, waited as he slid in and shut his. The car was immaculate, as she would expect. There was just a whisper of Boudreaux's expensive, understated cologne in the air, and not a gum wrapper or leaf in sight.

As Boudreaux started the car, Maggie put his switchblade in the glove compartment and gently shut the door. When she looked over at him, he was staring at her.

"What?" she asked.

"Your seat belt, please," he said.

They both buckled up, and Boudreaux pulled smoothly out of the parking lot and headed for the one red light at Hwy 98, which was called Main Street in town.

"Where are we going?" she asked him, as they turned right.

"Just outside Chipley," he said.

"Chipley!" she said. "That's an hour away."

"Yes. Do you need to be somewhere?"

Maggie looked out her window. "Not really," she said.

They rode in silence for the next several minutes. Maggie glanced over at Boudreaux and thought it almost interesting, the way she was only now seeing this other layer of his, this tightly coiled, carefully controlled danger that everyone else was aware of all along, but which she had never really felt from him, despite the fact that he intimidated her on several levels.

She also noticed that he seemed preoccupied for the first time since they'd started this odd relationship of sorts. One of the most compelling things about Boudreaux was that he had a knack for giving a person his complete and undivided attention, sometimes to the point of discomfort.

But today, he was focused on something either outside the car, or something deep within himself. She wondered if he had a string slowly unraveling, too.

As they drove out of town, Maggie could see the bay through Boudreaux's window, and she longed to be on it. They passed her parents' home, and she longed to be there, too. She wondered if Boudreaux would stop the car and let her out if she asked, but she didn't ask.

They pulled into the BP station just outside town, and up to the pump. Boudreaux got out, slid a credit card into the slot, and then started the pump. Maggie noticed that he got the premium gasoline. He shut his door from the outside and leaned in. "Excuse me for a moment, please," he said, and she watched him walk into the station.

A large stretch of empty land across the highway obstructed her view of the bay, so Maggie sat and stared at the scrub pines in the lot next to the station. She considered getting out of the car and refusing to go anywhere with Boudreaux, then felt silly for it. She did, in fact, have a large- caliber weapon on her, and she wasn't doing anything she hadn't made a conscious decision to do.

Boudreaux appeared at her window, a can of RC in one hand, a 7-Up in the other. "Which would you prefer?"

Maggie reached out and took the RC, and set it on her lap as Boudreaux put the gas pump away. The can of RC made her feel, stupidly, as though David were with her, and it felt silly to be comforted, but she was, all the same. Everything was turning inside out. She was sad and she was scared and Wyatt was angry with her. She swallowed as she thought how much she would like to be out on David's shrimp boat, discussing it all with him. It would be so easy, as it had always been.

"Thank you," she said to Boudreaux, as he got back in the car and started the engine.

"You're welcome," he said politely.

He put the 7-Up in the cup holder of the console, and Maggie popped her top, closed her eyes as she took a swallow of something as familiar and important to her as coffee. Then she put her can in the console as well.

They didn't speak again until they were outside town limits.

"Do you mind if I put the windows down?" Boudreaux asked with his usual impeccable manners. "I don't really care for air conditioning."

"No," she said to her window as it slid silently downward.

Thick, soupy air blew into the car as Boudreaux sped along, going just over the speed limit.

He was quiet again, and Maggie let him be. She watched him as he drove with his wrist resting lightly on the steering wheel. The sun glinted on the straight, brown hairs on his knuckles, and the hand looked far more relaxed than the owner. His lips were pressed together, making his slight overbite more pronounced, and Maggie could see his heartbeat in the artery on his neck.

Still, it struck her fresh how attractive he was physically, and how charismatic personally. If he were thirty years younger and there was no Wyatt, she realized that she could probably fall for the man, despite everything she knew, and she was glad that those circumstances didn't exist. It was bad enough that she was voluntarily riding in a car with a man that she knew had chopped a body into pieces and thrown it into the ocean. It was bad enough that she had liked him, anyway.

"What did you tell Tomlinson?" she asked after a good forty minutes of silence.

"I told him the truth," Boudreaux said. "But only as much of it as he needed to know."

He sighed, and looked over at her for the first time since they'd left the gas station. "I don't buy human beings," he said.

"Then why were you there?"

"To receive them," he said.

"I don't know what that means," Maggie said.

"They paid for someone to transport them here. I was giving them somewhere to go."

"Who brought them?"

"I don't know their names," he said. "I know the name of their boat, and I gave it to Tomlinson."

"Why did they just dump them in the water like that?" Maggie demanded.

"How the hell do I know, Maggie?" he snapped, glaring at her. Then he took a breath and looked back at the road. "I don't know," he said more quietly. "They were supposed to bring them within a couple of nautical miles of the island. They were also supposed to have compasses and two dinghies."

Maggie looked out her window and huffed out a breath. Scrub pines, date palms, and the occasional live oak whizzed past her window, and even at sixty or seventy miles per hour, she could hear the cicadas signaling from the woods.

They rode in silence for another fifteen or twenty minutes, passing through and around towns even smaller than Apalach, and with a lot less going for them. Here and there were huge parcels of land covered in corn, watermelons, or tobacco.

Finally, Boudreaux pulled off onto a gravel road with a metal cattle fence and a small sign announcing their arrival at Orange Blossom Farm, although no one grew oranges this far north.

They followed the road for almost a mile, and Maggie looked out at fields of tomatoes, corn, green beans, and what looked like sweet potatoes. In some of the fields, rows of vegetables were punctuated by dark-skinned people in wide-brimmed hats, picking produce and dropping it into five-gallon buckets.

Boudreaux parked in a gravel lot rimmed by an office trailer, a couple of hangar-sized warehouses, and several refrigerated trucks. Beyond the office trailer, about a hundred yards back, were several small houses.

He and Maggie got out, and they both stretched their backs a bit. The trailer door opened, and a Hispanic man of about fifty came down the metal stairs, smiling.

"¡Hola, Señor Boudreaux!" the man said as he walked toward him.

"¡Hola, Octavio!" Boudreaux answered, and Maggie followed him to meet Octavio halfway. "¿Como está todo?" Boudreaux asked as they shook hands.

"Everything is good, sir," Octavio said, then smiled at Maggie.

"Maggie, this is Octavio Gayoso, the farm manager," Boudreaux said. "Octavio, this is Maggie Redmond."

"Mucho gusto," Maggie said, and held out her hand.

"Mucho gusto," Octavio said back, shaking her hand gently.

"How are the tomatoes coming?" Boudreaux asked.

Octavio shrugged a shoulder. "Ah, *las tomates* want more rain, *si*? But the beans are good now."

Boudreaux started walking, and Octavio fell in step with him. Maggie followed a pace behind. "Any more problems with the Walmart guy?" Boudreaux asked.

"No, he does not seem to need to negotiate anymore," Octavio said. "And he was much more *simpático* on the phone."

"Good." Boudreaux put a hand on the man's shoulder. "We won't keep you, Octavio. I'm just going to show Maggie around a little."

"Si, está bien," Octavio said. He smiled at Maggie. "It was good to meet you."

"Good to meet you," Maggie answered.

Octavio walked back toward the office trailer, and Maggie followed Boudreaux as he started on a gravel road that wound around back toward the houses. There were about a dozen of them, small cottages, really, set up on cement blocks rather than poured foundations. Beyond the houses, Maggie could see another dozen or so singlewide trailers, some of them FEMA trailers, some not.

The little houses were older, but they looked to be in decent shape. Most of them had pots or coffee cans of flowers on the front steps, and in a big patch of grass in the center were several plastic riding toys and a sandbox.

Two women in their twenties sat on overturned buckets, watching several small children play. One of the women was nursing an infant, its legs sticking out from under a woven nursing blanket. The women looked at Maggie and Boudreaux curiously. One of them raised a hand to them, and Boudreaux raised one back. Then he put his hands in his pockets as he and Maggie stopped underneath a small date palm.

"The girl on the left, and I admit I don't remember her name, is Octavio's daughter. That's his first grandson," Boudreaux said.

"Where are they from?"

"Miami," he said.

"I meant originally," she said flatly.

"Honduras. They've been in the US for twelve years." He looked at her. "They're naturalized."

Maggie watched him as he looked around the little residential area. "It's not fancy by any means, but there are no rats, and there's plumbing and air conditioning and water." He looked over at her. "You'd be surprised how unusual that actually is."

"Does everyone who works here live here?"

"No, but most of them do. It's cheaper. They pay a flat rate for rent and utilities and the rent's about half what they'd pay in town. I only charge what I need to cover the utilities. It's the only way I can afford to pay them."

He looked over at Maggie. "I won't pretend they have it made here, but they have it better than at most farms," he said. "Most places pay less than minimum wage, under the table. They set quotas that are almost impossible to meet, then dock wages when the quotas aren't met."

He watched as two little girls wandered over to the sandbox and started pushing little cars through the sand. "I pay minimum wage and give small bonuses for exceeding quota. It's not perfect, but it's the best I can do. Agriculture doesn't pay farms enough to pay the wages workers ought to be earning," he said. "Some farms underpay to a disgusting degree and some outright steal from their workers. A lot of the people who work here came from farms where they actually owed their employers money."

Maggie turned her gaze from the little girls and looked at him. "Did any of them come from Guatemala?"

"Yes," he said, still watching the girls.

"Is that something you do regularly?"

He looked at her, his eyes almost challenging. "I've done it before, yes. I'll likely do it again, and I won't apologize for it."

Maggie looked back at the young women.

"Have you ever been to Guatemala, Maggie?"

"No."

"I have. Thirty years of civil war and they still have nothing. Almost nobody owns their own land, and those that do can't get a decent price for what they manage to grow out of dirt that's almost too poor to grow anything." He looked back at the kids playing in the grass. "The government's corrupt as hell and hates its own people. Almost every family has at least one relative in prison."

Maggie looked over at him. "What were you doing in Guatemala?"

"Catholic missions trips," he said, and Maggie would have laughed if anyone else had said it. She knew he took his Catholicism very seriously, however he managed that.

"Let's go," he said, and turned back toward the parking area. Maggie followed, running a couple of steps to catch up.

"That's it? We drove an hour to spend three minutes here?" she asked him.

"You want to look at the books? Inspect one of the houses?" he asked her. "You've seen what I brought you here to see, but if you want to wait until everyone comes in from the fields so you can interview them, we can. But it doesn't get dark til 8:30."

They walked in silence back to the car and got in. Boudreaux stared out the windshield a moment, and Maggie watched him.

"Why did you bring me here?" she asked him.

He continued to stare out the windshield just long enough for her to start thinking he wasn't going to answer. Then he looked over at her. "You might find this ironic, but I don't like being suspected of something I wouldn't do."

"Why do you care what I think?"

He looked at her for a long time, and she thought she saw several different answers pass across his eyes. "I respect you. I'd like that respect to be mutual, on some level."

He put on his seat belt, and she did the same, then he started the car and turned it around in the lot. Maggie looked back out her window as they pulled back onto the road and headed south again.

NINE

Boudreaux and Maggie rode in silence for several minutes, each wrapped up in their own thoughts.

Maggie was having trouble keeping hers straight. She'd been angry with Boudreaux on the way out to Chipley, and deeply disappointed, as much as that troubled her. Now she wasn't sure what to think. Her gut said that he was being honest with her about his involvement with the poor Guatemalans, but she was experiencing some distrust of her gut these days.

Half an hour into their drive back, Maggie's cell buzzed at her and she pulled it out of her back pocket. It was Sky.

"Hey, baby," Maggie answered. It felt surreal to be talking to her child in Boudreaux's car.

"Hey, Mom," Sky said. "We just got back to Grandma and Granddad's and I wanted to know if I could go spend the night with Bella. She's got a couple of Redbox movies."

"What about Kyle?"

"He wants to stay here with Granddad. They're gonna play corn hole out back."

"Well, I guess that's okay," Maggie said, simultaneously relieved and disappointed. She felt separated from her family, and she had looked forward to being home and re-grounding herself. "How'd it go today?"

"Dude. Have you even been outside?" Sky asked. "The oysters were cooked already when we pulled 'em up. But we got a full bag, plus our bucket. We're having them for dinner."

"That sounds nice," Maggie said.

"Where are you?"

"I'm on my way back to town. I'm working on a case."

"The people from Guatemala?" Sky asked, sounding a little more subdued.

"Yeah."

"Did that little boy like the stuff you took him?"

"I don't know. He was asleep," Maggie answered.

"Poor kid. That whole thing totally sucks."

"Yeah, it does."

"All right, so it's okay if I go?"

"Yeah, it's okay. Tell Kyle to call me before he goes to bed," Maggie said.

"You don't want me to call you before I go to bed?" Sky said, teasing in her voice.

"You'll be going to bed at 3 a.m. If you call me, you're grounded."

"Okay. Later, dude."

"Later, dude," Maggie said.

She disconnected the call and set the phone in her lap. When she looked over at Boudreaux, he was looking at her.

"You're a good mother," he said.

The compliment embarrassed her, and she shrugged. "On my good days."

"Was David a good father?"

Maggie felt a clenching in her chest. "Yes. Very good."

"Even though he started running pot?" Boudreaux said it without judgment in his voice.

"Yes."

"But you couldn't stay married to him."

It took Maggie a moment to answer, to admit to something she'd like to take back. "No."

Boudreaux was quiet for a moment, watched the road. "I hope he was able to redeem himself somewhat in your eyes," he said quietly.

Maggie looked down at the warm can of RC in the console. "Yes. He was."

"Redemption is elusive," he said.

Maggie started to say something, but her phone buzzed again. It was Wyatt. She took a deep breath and answered.

"Hey," she said.

"Hey. Where are you?"

"I'm, uh, on my way back to town."

"From where?"

"Chipley."

"Never heard of it," Wyatt answered.

"Neither have most of the people who live there," she said.

"What were you doing in Chipley?"

"Checking out Boudreaux's farm," she said.

"Huh," Wyatt said after a moment. "I'm wondering how you're traveling, because your Jeep is here at Boss. I'd appreciate it if you said by spaceship."

"No." Maggie bit the corner of her lip. "I'm with Boudreaux."

There was a long pause on the line and Maggie grew more nervous as she waited.

"Well then," Wyatt finally said. "That's just Jim damn Dandy."

Maggie looked at her phone and saw that he had indeed hung up on her. She dropped it back onto her lap and sighed.

"That didn't sound like it went over too well," Boudreaux said.

"No." Maggie looked out of her window at the unrelenting miles of tall, skinny scrub pines. "But he was already upset with me."

"I guess you told him about Gregory and Sport."

"Yes."

"And me." Boudreaux said it matter-of-factly.

"Yes." Maggie sighed. "Wyatt wasn't exactly happy about me keeping so many things to myself."

"We men aren't that fond of finding out that we don't know as much as we believe we know."

"Professionally, he had every right to know."

"I agree. But I'm willing to bet that he's more upset personally than professionally."

"I don't know," Maggie said. "Secrecy's kind of a new thing for me. With that one exception."

She was afraid that would lead to more discussion of Gregory. Or of David, and she didn't have the heart for either topic. She looked over at Boudreaux. "What about you? Do you keep secrets from your wife?"

"No," he said smoothly, watching the road. "She knows that I can't stand her."

⚓　⚓　⚓

They got back to the parking lot at Boss Oyster a little before six, and Boudreaux pulled in next to Maggie's Jeep. She got out, and looked at Boudreaux through the open window.

"Thank you for coming with me," he said, sounding tired.

Maggie nodded, then glanced over at a local couple coming out of the raw bar. They looked over at her, and Maggie felt her career and her reputation taking their last breaths. She was almost too drained to care.

"Goodnight, Mr. Boudreaux," she said.

"Goodnight, Maggie."

Maggie got in her Jeep and watched Boudreaux back out, then she looked around at the parking lot. She had almost hoped that Wyatt's car would be there, but it wasn't.

She sat for a minute, gathering her nerve, then pulled out her cell and dialed Wyatt's number. He answered on the first ring.

"Hey," he said.

"Hey," Maggie said. "I know you're angry with me and you probably don't feel like talking to me right now, but could we please? Anyway?"

"We need to do that, yes," he answered.

"Thank you," she said. "What are you doing right now?"

She heard Wyatt sigh.

"I'm sitting on the steps with Stoopid," he answered.

⚓ ⚓ ⚓

When Maggie pulled up in front of her house ten minutes later, Stoopid had apparently become bored with Wyatt. Coco had not. She was standing near his feet, smiling, until Maggie parked the car, then she barreled over, eyes wide and tongue lolling, and collapsed at Maggie's feet as she got out of the Jeep.

Stoopid flailed over from near the chicken yard, apprised Maggie of the fact that Wyatt was present, then ran back from whence he'd come, neck feathers at half-mast.

Wyatt sat on the third step, a six pack of Yuengling on the step beside him. He was drinking one of them. He stood up as Maggie walked toward the house with Coco on her heels.

"Hey," Maggie said.

"Hey," he said back.

They looked at each other a moment, then he picked up the six-pack and stepped aside as she came up the stairs. She stopped a couple of steps up from him, looked him eye to eye. He looked tired and closed off from her, and she was surprised that she could feel that in a physical way.

"I just need to take a quick shower, okay? Five minutes?" she asked.

He nodded at her. "You want a beer?"

"No, thanks," she said, as they started up the stairs again. "I don't actually like beer. I just drink it if there's nothing else."

"You need to fix these stairs," Wyatt said behind her.

"I know."

She opened the front door and stood aside for Wyatt.

"I'll just sit on the deck," he said.

Maggie faltered for a moment, then nodded. "Okay. I'll be right out."

Coco followed her inside, and Maggie quickly got out of her sticky clothes and into the shower. She tended to linger in the shower until the hot water was gone, but this time she was out in less than five minutes. She'd spent the entire time dreading the upcoming conversation and trying to come up with justifications for her actions, but she wasn't so far gone that she could find any.

She threw on some khaki shorts and a white tee shirt, poured a glass of Muscadine wine, and walked out to the living room. Coco was sitting at the sliding glass door, vibrating at Wyatt, who was sitting at the small round table outside.

He looked up when she walked out onto the deck, and she had an urge to curl up on his lap. She remembered what that had felt like. It had felt safe, and it had felt right.

Instead, she sat down in the chair across from him. Coco sat in the middle, but it was Wyatt she was smiling at. Wyatt wasn't smiling. Maggie was glad she got a good swallow of wine before he spoke.

"Did I ever tell you about when Lily told me she had cancer?"

That threw Maggie. "No."

He sighed. "It was three weeks *after* she decided to have a lumpectomy instead of a mastectomy," he said. "She told me two days before she went in for the surgery."

Maggie had no idea what to say to that. He looked up at her. "I realize it was her body and it was her cancer, but it was our lives, and I had no idea. No idea at all, until it was too late for me to have any say in it."

"I'm not sure what to say," Maggie said. "I'm sorry."

Wyatt took a long pull of his beer, then banged the bottle down on the table, making both Maggie and Coco jump just a little.

"I don't want you to be sorry," he said. "I want you to trust me enough to be honest."

"I get what you're—" she started.

"No, you probably don't," he said. He stood up and took a couple of paces, then stood with his hands on his hips. "I understand why you didn't tell me about the rape, and I understand why you felt like you couldn't tell me about Gregory Boudreaux. But Wilmette? And Boudreaux, freaking Boudreaux!"

"I told you because I do trust you, Wyatt!" Maggie said. "I know I waited too long, but I told you. I don't want to have secrets."

"But you do, Maggie." Wyatt glanced at Coco, who had stopped smiling and was looking confused. He lowered his voice when he spoke again. "You do. Because I don't know what the hell is going on with you and Boudreaux."

"I don't either, but it's not—it's not a romantic thing, if that's what you're thinking," she said.

"That's not what I'm worried about, but I wouldn't be too sure of that if I were you."

"That's not it, Wyatt," she said.

"Then tell me what the hell it is!" he yelled.

Coco whined and stood up, and Maggie put a hand on her neck before she stood up, too. Sitting made her feel too small.

"I don't know."

"Well, you need to figure it out, because you just took a road trip with the guy that *you* told me chopped up Wilmette and dumped him in the ocean."

"Look, I know you don't get it, but I really don't think he wants to hurt me," she said.

"That's not even the point." Wyatt bent over a little so she could look him in the eye. "You're a cop. You're a mom. You coach girls' softball, dammit! But you voluntarily got in a car with a guy that chops people up."

Maggie shook her head. "I know. I *know*."

"I want to go over there and shoot him because he's messing with your head!" he yelled.

"Everything is messing with my head!" she yelled back. "Are you kidding me? In the space of a month, I work the suicide of the guy that raped me, find out the foot in my other case belonged to the guy that watched it happen, I get caught up in some kind of weirdness with Boudreaux, and I watch my ex-husband get blown up right in front of me! You're damn right something's messing with my head, but it's not just Boudreaux!"

Coco whined and licked Maggie's hand, then stretched her neck and nudged Wyatt's. He reached down and put a hand on her head, then ran the hand through his hair.

"You put me in a position of having to choose between protecting your privacy and doing my job, Maggie, and you did it at least partly because of this thing with you and Boudreaux."

"That's not true! I told you as soon as I knew for sure that he killed Wilmette."

"Now you're not even being honest with yourself," Wyatt said. "How long did you suspect he did it?"

Maggie paused, not because she didn't want to answer, but because she wasn't sure what the answer was. "I don't know," she finally said. "But I needed to be sure."

"And now you are, and you're riding around the countryside with him like he's your real estate agent!"

"It was about the Guatemalans, Wyatt, the one case I can still touch with a ten foot pole!"

"But riding in his car was not about the Guatemalans, Maggie. It was about you and Boudreaux!"

"Look, I realize that doesn't seem like the smart thing to do—"

"Smart thing? It doesn't even seem like the normal thing to do," he shot back.

Maggie felt a coldness pass through her chest, and she took a deep breath. "I'm as normal as I need to be," she said. "And I'm sorry that I put you in a bad position, and I'm sorry that this is getting in the way of something that has barely even gotten started—"

"Don't kid yourself, Maggie. This," Wyatt said, and pointed at her and back at himself. "This has been going on a lot longer than a month and you know it."

"I don't want to fight with you," Maggie said.

"Well, that's too bad! I fight when I'm mad!" Wyatt said. "People fight."

"David and I never fought," she said, and instantly regretted it. She hadn't meant it to be a dig, she just wasn't used to arguing this way.

"Of course you didn't, Maggie," Wyatt said. "You guys were practically brother and sister."

Maggie stared at him, and he huffed out a breath and started walking toward the stairs.

"Where are you going?" Maggie asked, following him, her vision blurred by sudden tears.

Wyatt turned around on the stairs, but he didn't look at her. "That was a crappy thing to say, and if we're going to start saying crappy things, it's time for me to leave," he said. He started back down the stairs. "I didn't come here to hurt you."

"What did you come here for?" she called after him.

He stopped and turned around. "I came here to fix it, dammit," he said.

"Then let's fix it," she said.

"I can't fix it, Maggie! You need to fix it." He took a few steps across the gravel, then turned around and put his hands on his hips. "Let me tell you something, lady. I didn't care whether Lily had one breast, two breasts, or no breasts. I would have loved her anyway."

Then he stalked to his car and got in, and Maggie and Coco watched him turn around and drive down the road, away from them, and into the twilight.

CHAPTER

TEN

A brick pathway led from Boudreaux's back patio to the guest cottage in which Amelia and Miss Evangeline resided.

Boudreaux's loafers made little sound as he followed the walkway, walking between various colors of hibiscus and hydrangea. The breeze had picked up, and rattled through the trees like someone was hitting the leaves with sticks.

A rectangular shaft of light from the open screen door cut into the darkness of the back yard, and Boudreaux could hear the tinny sounds of the television floating through the open windows.

Boudreaux stepped onto the patio. He could see Miss Evangeline, clad in a fluffy yellow robe, sitting in her cushioned rocker in the living area. He tapped at the screen door, and she looked over at the door, the lamplight making her eyeglass lenses appear to be solid white.

"Amelia, open the door Mr. Benny," she called. There was no answer. "Amelia!"

When there was still no answer, Miss Evangeline made as though to struggle out of her chair.

"It's not locked. You want me to just come in?" Boudreaux asked.

She waved at him and settled back down, though she hadn't made appreciable progress in rising, anyway. Boudreaux opened the screen door and stepped inside.

The cottage was small and cozy, in a Florida vacation sort of way, with wicker furniture and lots of plants and bright, tropical prints. There was a small kitchenette in one corner of the living area, and there was one bedroom off of each side of the main room.

"I don't know where that girl at," Miss Evangeline said.

Boudreaux pointed toward Amelia's room. "The shower's running," he said.

"What?" she barked.

"The shower, she's in the shower," he said.

"What you doin', Mr. Benny?" she asked.

"I'm just getting back," he said. "I wanted to talk to you about something."

"Move my basket, sit down there," she said.

Boudreaux picked up a small basket of crochet projects, set it on the coffee table, and took a seat on the wicker loveseat. A nature documentary was on the TV. "Do you mind if I turn this down?" he asked.

"Turn what down?" she asked.

He picked up the remote and lowered the volume, then rested his elbows on his knees and looked at her. "I have a problem."

"You got more than one," she said matter-of-factly.

"That's true. But I'm talking about Patrick," he said.

Miss Evangeline made that little clicking sound with her tongue that she made when she was irritated. "That boy a fool," she said.

Boudreaux nodded. "Yes. But he's become a dangerous fool."

"That boy a danger nobody but his own self," she said.

"Do you remember the man they found in the burning boat? In the newspaper?"

Miss Evangeline looked over at him, her eyes squinting behind her thick lenses as she thought. "The drug dealer man. I say good riddance, me."

"Yes. But I think he also tried to kill Maggie," he said quietly.

Miss Evangeline stared at him a moment, and he looked away from her gaze, focused on the TV Guide on the coffee table.

"What he do it for?"

"It's a long story," he answered. "He's trying to cover his tracks."

"You don't kill him already?" she asked.

"He's been in Tallahassee since then, at some legal symposium," Boudreaux said. "I haven't seen him."

"He ain't all stupid, then," she answered after a moment. "I be in Cuba, me, I done this. I don't be around nowhere."

"I think he's losing it," Boudreaux said.

"He losing what?"

Bennett tapped at one of his temples.

"That boy broke when you got him, Mr. Benny," she said. "He already broke."

"I've been thinking a lot lately about nature versus nurture," he said.

"I don't know what it mean," she said.

"It means—"

"I don't say I *need* to know what it mean," she interrupted. "Don't matter. That armadillo-lookin' woman, she ruin them boy long 'fore you marry her. T'ree year old, he already ruin, think the moon rise out between his butt cheeks, him."

"Craig's not so bad," Boudreaux said of his younger stepson, though he wondered if that was because Craig was barely part of the family anymore.

"That only 'cause he got no spine," Miss Evangeline said. "She yank the spine right out *that* one early."

Boudreaux sighed and looked over at her. "I'm obliged to fix this in some way."

"What you do?" she asked.

"I don't know. That's why I'm back here talking to you," Boudreaux said. "I want you to give me some advice, but not based on the fact that you don't like him."

"Like, don't like, don't matter, no," she said. "What I always tell you?"

"Family," he answered quietly. "Everything is for family."

"For true," she said. "You do what you got to do for your family, you."

"It's partly my fault."

"Ain't nothin' Mr. Benny fault," she snapped. "Boy do what he do. You fix it 'cause you got to."

Boudreaux nodded, as Miss Evangeline squinted at the TV.

"Why these people talk so low?" she said. "I can't understand nothin' what they say."

Boudreaux stared at the coffee table. "Pray for me," he said quietly.

"I all the time pray for you," she answered, looking at the TV. "Lord wore out from hearin' 'bout Mr. Benny. These people talk like they don't want me know what they say."

Boudreaux picked up the remote and turned up the volume, then put it in her hands, kissed her temple, and headed for the door.

⚓ ⚓ ⚓

Maggie lay on the bed, the quilt thrown back and nothing but a sheet covering her. She listened to the steady *swish* of Coco's breathing beside her, and the crickets and frogs competing for audience outside her open windows. Every now and then, something would make them go quiet, and she would hold her breath and listen for a creaking of wood that shouldn't be there, or the snap of a twig. It was an old habit, and one she didn't anticipate breaking.

She never heard anything out of place as she lay there, at least nothing more disturbing than her own thoughts.

For a woman of fairly strong thoughts and opinions, she'd had very little to say that night to Wyatt. She couldn't justify driving off with Boudreaux. She couldn't reconcile her actions of recent weeks with the woman and mother and cop she'd always thought she'd been. And while she'd been hurt and then angered by what Wyatt had said about her and David, once left alone, she had thought about that most of all.

It was like someone had taken the tarp off of something and shown her that she hadn't really known what was underneath, like she'd thought it was a car and Wyatt had said that it was a boat. First she'd denied, because she knew better than anyone what her marriage was. But some slow moving tentacle had started swirling and undulating inside her until she'd realized, with a sharp intake of breath, that Wyatt hadn't really been that far off.

She'd loved David, deeply, and still did. He occupied some place in almost all of her memories. But when she sifted through them, lying there in the bed that they had shared, she could not remember ever actually falling in love with him.

CHAPTER

ELEVEN

E arly the next morning, Wyatt sat at his desk, a cold cup of coffee beside him.

He pecked at the keyboard of his computer, clicking from one page to the next, asking the computer to print out each page as he went. He'd have gotten to it the morning after Maggie had told him what Charlie Harper had said to her, if it hadn't been for the Guatemalans.

When the printer finally stopped humming, he had a sheaf of papers in his hands. He divided them up by name.

The niggling thought had come to him when Maggie had told him. He'd remembered being frustrated that they'd not been able to find a connection between Rupert Fain, of recent burning boat fame, and Charlie Harper, the man who had tried to kill Maggie, and presumably succeeded with David.

It had reminded him of something poking at his mind from when he'd been in Gainesville, trying to find Fain after he'd melted his middleman, Myron Graham, into a pile of bones and patchwork leather. It was Myron Graham that had been niggling at him for the last few days.

He organized the printouts by name, dividing them into three small stacks. Rupert Fain, Myron Graham, Charlie Harper.

As far as anyone knew, Rupert Fain had never lived in Franklin County. But Charlie Harper had lived in Eastpoint right up until the moment that Wyatt had put a .40 caliber round in his chest. Myron Graham had lived in Eastpoint until 2009, then moved on to Gainesville, where he was hired by Rupert Fain and got on the path to a career as a chicken fried steak.

They had all done time, but not in the same facility or at the same time. There was a connection between Graham and Fain. But there was no known connection between Graham and Harper, or Harper and Fain.

Wyatt pulled the truncated, one-page arrest and conviction report from each stack and laid them in a neat row, then looked at each one. After a few minutes, he sighed.

There was a very simple reason why they couldn't find a connection between Fain and Harper or Harper and Graham. There wasn't one.

Wyatt stood up, grabbed his SO ball cap and Harper's info sheet, and stalked out of the office.

⚓ ⚓ ⚓

Maggie tapped on the hotel room door, and Tomlinson opened it a moment later, smelling of hotel soap and with still-damp hair.

"Morning, Lieutenant," he said as he stood back to let her in.

"Good morning, Agent Tomlinson," she answered. She glanced over at the bedroom area, where Virgilio was sitting on the end of one of the made beds, wearing an outfit that Kyle had worn to her birthday dinner last year, when everything was normal. He was drinking a small carton of orange juice and watching Dora the Explorer, which Maggie found almost funny.

The blond female agent wasn't there, but a young, prematurely balding man with glasses was sitting in an armchair near the front door.

"Do you mind if I say hello?" Maggie asked Tomlinson.

"No, not at all," he said. "Go ahead."

Maggie walked to the back of the suite and stopped by the bed. Virgilio glanced up at her, then looked back at the TV. "¡Hola, Virgilio!" Maggie said.

He looked back up at her. "¡Hola, señora!" he answered in a small voice.

"Me llama Maggie," she said. "¿Te acuerdas?" *Do you remember?*

The little boy shook his head slowly, and Maggie struggled for something to say now that she was there. I'm sorry? I care? She was a stranger; he didn't care about either.

"¿Necesitas algo?" *Do you need anything?*

"No," he said politely.

Maggie nodded and watched Dora dancing with her irritating monkey for a moment while she tried to think of something else to say. She came up empty.

"Okay, está bien," she said finally. "Nos vemos." *See you later.*

Virgilio looked up at her, but didn't reply, and Maggie walked back over to Tomlinson. He was sitting at the small round table near the window, and she sat down in the other chair.

"So, here's where we are," he said. "We got people in Guatemala in contact with the kid's grandparents. His father's people," he added. "We don't have a single ID for anyone else on that boat besides Virgilio's family."

"Isn't that unusual?" Maggie asked. "Wouldn't they want some kind of ID, to try to get visas or green cards or something?"

"That depends on their situations, Lieutenant," he answered. "You get deported back to Mexico for trotting over to Texas, you'll probably do some jail time. You get deported back to Guatemala, especially if you're in trouble with the government or the military police, you're gonna be really sorry you got sent home. Equally importantly, your family's gonna be sorry."

Maggie sighed. "So what happens to Virgilio?"

"We don't know that yet," he answered. "But we do know this: Guatemala doesn't want these bodies back."

"What?"

"They don't want the hassle, the expense or the local publicity," he said.

"I should think they would want the publicity," she said. "See how these people failed? See what happens?"

"In some cases, that might be useful. But we don't know who these people are. There's no CODIS in Guatemala," he said, referring to the DNA database. "Half these people have probably never even been fingerprinted. Some of them probably never even got birth certificates. They're of no real use to the government and they represent a significant pain in the ass."

"I don't understand. What happens to the—what happens to them?"

"I'm still working on that," he answered.

Maggie blew out a breath. "Where are you on the people that brought them here?"

"We're making progress on that front," he answered. "Bennett Boudreaux gave us the name of the boat. We're running down ownership, which appears to be a little convoluted, and trying to track down the boat itself."

"How *was* your talk with Boudreaux?" she asked.

"That's an interesting guy you have there," he said.

"Yeah, we're aware," she said. "But what did he tell you?"

"Said his only involvement was that he was in contact with a priest from time to time, and every now and again, this priest knew of locals who had paid for passage to Florida or Alabama or Mississippi. When they came here, Boudreaux took care of them, got 'em situated."

"So what's going to happen to Boudreaux?" she asked.

"Not a thing, so far as I can see."

"Why not?"

"Well, for one thing, he doesn't give a rat's ass, pardon the expression, whether I threaten him with federal prosecution. That man's as Catholic as they come. He's not giving the name of the priest and he didn't even actually say the priest was a facilitator in all this, or if he just knows what's going on."

"So who is running it over there?"

Tomlinson rubbed at his face. "These guys with the boat probably have people working there. For all we know, the priest hears about this stuff during confession. We're not talking about some Catholic Charities human trafficking operation."

"But Boudreaux's still doing something illegal, right?"

"Sure. If we had proof, which we don't," he said. "And if he didn't have so many senators and congressmen as friends, which he does."

Maggie shook her head. "Wow," she said quietly.

"Yeah. Well, listen. If he was paying by the head for these people to be brought over, and then putting them to work, we'd probably have more leeway, since that's akin to slavery right there." Tomlinson coughed into his fist. "But he says the only thing he paid out was diesel. He sent a boat out to their coordinates off of Louisiana to refuel them."

Maggie stood up. "Okay. Well." She held out her hand. "I'll talk to you later, I guess."

"You bet," he said, standing to shake her hand.

He closed the hotel room door behind her, and she stood on the second-story walkway, unavoidably faced with the river. The morning sun glinted off of it like there were diamonds just below the surface, and the smaller boats in the marina bobbed gently in the wake of a large Chris Craft center console that was headed out to the bay.

Maggie chewed her lip for a moment, then pulled out her cell phone.

"Hey, Sunshine," her dad answered.

"Hey, Daddy. You care if I take the runabout out for a little bit?"

"Where you headed?"

"Just out to, uh…just out past the Reserve," she answered, referring to the State Reserve at the eastern tip of St. George Island. She knew her father understood what she meant.

He paused for just a moment, and when he answered, his voice was even gentler than usual. "You got the fuel for it," he said.

⚓ ⚓ ⚓

Wyatt turned off of Twin Lakes Road in Eastpoint, not that far from the Sheriff's Office, and onto a gravel road that divided two rows of rundown trailers.

The last trailer on the right was a gray singlewide with light blue trim, and accent colors of rust and black mold. A Chevelle that would have been worth something if it had paint, a hood, and one more tire sat in the gravel driveway.

A battered 80s-era Corolla sat next to it. Wyatt pulled in behind the Chevelle and shut off the engine.

In front of the trailer, there was an old wooden cable spool being used as a table, with three aluminum folding chairs arranged around it. In one of them sat a very pretty girl in her mid-twenties, with long dark hair pulled into a ponytail, and equally long, tan legs stretched out in front of her.

She looked up as Wyatt got out of the cruiser, and he saw a flicker of interest or surprise cross her face as she took a drag off of her cigarette. Then she looked down at her bare feet and wiggled her toes as Wyatt walked up to the table. Three bottles of nail polish sat on the table next to a pack of Maverick cigarettes, a peace sign lighter, and a plastic cup holding what looked like Kool-Aid.

"Hi," Wyatt said pleasantly. "Are you Carrie Fleming?"

The girl looked up at him, squinting against the sun. "Yeah?"

On closer inspection, she was less pretty than she obviously used to be. She was a little underweight, and it made the planes of her face too sharp. Her gray eyes had dirty yellow smudges beneath them, and there was a fresh scar just beneath her lower lip.

"I'm Sheriff Hamilton," Wyatt said. "Can I talk to you for a minute?"

He ran his finger along a wet condensation ring in front of the empty chair beside her. When he looked back at the girl, she was trying to fix a slightly flirtatious look onto her face that made him sad for her.

"That depends," she answered. "I haven't done any-thing, and Charlie's dead, dude."

"Yeah, well, I wanted to ask you some questions about Charlie, anyway." He gave her one of his dimpled smiles, the polite one. "If you have a minute."

Her eyes cut over to the trailer door for a second, then she shrugged. Wyatt sat down in the chair beside her as she crushed out her cigarette on the bottom of the cable spool, then picked up a bottle of light green nail polish and shook it.

"Is this Charlie's place or yours?" Wyatt asked.

"It's his. But nobody's asked for it back, and the rent's paid til the 15th." She opened the bottle and pulled a foot up onto the edge of her chair.

"How long you been living here?"

She focused on her pinky toe as she carefully slid some polish on it. "I don't know. Six months, maybe?" She glanced over at him and gave him part of a grin. "Why, you looking for a new place?"

Wyatt smiled in polite appreciation of her wit. "So, I guess you won't need to bother going to court about Charlie beating you up last month."

"No, but obviously I didn't kill him," she said to her toes.

"No, that was me," Wyatt said.

She looked up at him, and there was a new look in her eyes that depressed him a little. It wasn't so much surprise as it was titillation. "Yeah?" she asked.

Just then, the front door of the trailer opened, and a guy in jeans and a black tee shirt stepped out, a bottle of Bud in his hand. He hesitated on the top step when he saw Wyatt, then tried to blow it off as he walked down the metal steps.

He had thinning brown hair, despite being in his late twenties at the most. A small collection of hairs on his chin had been optimistically fashioned into a future goatee.

Carrie looked up at him as he stopped by the table. "Sheriff's talkin' to me about Charlie," she said.

The guy looked slightly relieved. "Well, I didn't know Charlie," he said.

"That's okay," Wyatt said. "I'm not here to talk to you."

"Well, should I sit back down or go back inside?" the guy asked, a slight, nervous grin on his face.

"Is that your Toyota?" Wyatt asked.

The guy shifted his feet. "Uh, yeah."

"Then why don't you set your beer down and go renew those tags real quick," Wyatt said with a smile.

"I've been meaning to do that, man, just been workin' weird hours," the guy said.

"Well, you're not working now," Wyatt offered helpfully.

"Uh, yeah. Sure." He put his beer down on the table and glanced at Carrie. "I'll be back in a little bit."

Carrie shrugged a shoulder and concentrated on her big toenail. The guy got in his car, and Wyatt watched him back out and head up the gravel road.

"That's Jesse Vickers, isn't it?" he asked the girl.

"Yeah," she said noncommittally.

"New boyfriend?"

Carrie looked over at him as she put the brush back in the bottle. "Maybe." She smiled. "Why?"

"Not much better than Charlie," Wyatt said. "You ever think about going for a guy that doesn't toss women around?"

"I don't meet a lot of nice guys," she said.

"Maybe you should try waiting more than ten minutes," Wyatt said kindly.

"Look, if you're interested, just say so and we'll talk," she said. "But if not, well, you're not my dad."

Wyatt nodded. "No, I'm not, on either count," he said. "But you could do better."

Carrie shrugged again, pulled her other foot up onto the chair, and grabbed the brush out of the polish bottle. She dabbed the sides a bit before applying it to her other big toe.

"Who hired Charlie to shoot Lieutenant Redmond?" Wyatt asked.

"You guys already asked me all that," she said. "I told you, I don't know anything about that. He didn't talk to me unless he wanted something or he was feeling mean."

"Well, somebody hired him."

"Maybe he just had it in for her," she said. "She's a cop."

"No. He might not like *us*, but he didn't know *her*."

"Well, I don't know what to tell you, dude."

"Somebody paid him $20,000 to kill a law enforcement officer."

She looked up at him sharply. "He didn't have no $20,000."

"That's 'cause he used it to pay his bail for knocking you around again," Wyatt said.

Carrie paused, nail brush in hand, and squinted over at him a moment. "That wasn't gonna go anywhere anyway," she said.

"Sure it was," Wyatt said. "And since Charlie was a two-time loser, he was gonna go back to State."

"No, he wasn't. His lawyer said it was gonna get dropped." She put the cap back on her polish and stretched her legs out in front of her to inspect her toes. "He couldn't wait to tell me that, either, like it wouldn't do me any good if the neighbors called the cops again."

"Why would the charges get dropped?" Wyatt asked.

"How do I know? Something about the cops didn't have a reason to come in the house."

"Said who?"

"The lawyer, dude. He said the DA or whatever was gonna drop the charges."

"Who's the lawyer?"

"Something Green."

"That's very helpful," Wyatt said, smiling. "You mind coming down to the station with me, just for a minute, to sign a statement to that effect?"

"To what effect?"

"Just what you've told me, about what the lawyer said."

"Can't you bring it here?"

"I'm asking you to do it there. Please." He gave her another smile.

She sighed. "Will you bring me home?"

"Actually, I need to be somewhere," he said. "But I'll have one of the deputies run you back. Half an hour, tops."

She sighed again. "Can you at least run me by the store on the way?" she asked. "I'm almost out of cigarettes."

"I can do that."

⚓ ⚓ ⚓

Boudreaux was sitting at the teak desk in his study. Light from the French doors out to the side porch cast rectangular patterns of day onto the desk and the wool rug on which it sat. The shafts of light were accompanied by very little else on the surface of the desk: a small Tiffany lamp, a piece of driftwood that had been made into a pen holder, a leather portfolio that held Boudreaux's appointment book and checkbooks.

Boudreaux sat back in his brown leather chair, fingers steepled beneath his chin, staring at an oil painting of shrimp boats headed out to sea.

His gaze shifted to the door from the hallway, as Patrick opened it and came inside. He closed the door behind him and stopped, looking at Boudreaux. He was dressed as impeccably as always, if a tad too much on the GQ side, but there were shadows beneath his eyes.

"I'm here," he said.

Boudreaux's left eye twitched almost invisibly, and he slowly straightened up and leaned his elbows on his desk. "Sit down," he said quietly.

"I'm on my way to work, so I don't have much time to chat," Patrick said, as he made his way to one of the leather armchairs in front of the desk.

"No, you don't," Boudreaux said flatly. He could see that Patrick was trying to amble, to walk as though he had no concerns, but he was failing.

Patrick glanced up at him as he sat, then looked away. "So what's up?" he asked.

Boudreaux took a cleansing breath, staring at Patrick as he did. Patrick attempted to meet his gaze, but held it for only a moment before he needed to look elsewhere.

"You've done a remarkably foolish thing, even for you," Boudreaux said.

Patrick threw an ankle onto his knee and fiddled with the cuff of his five-hundred dollar trousers. "Is this about the pot again, Pop?"

Patrick had admitted, almost proudly, that he had been the one to kill Myron Graham and steal Fain's pot, after Graham had told him he wouldn't be paying any more "commissions." He'd also been pretty proud that David Seward had taken the blame for it.

"It's about Fain," Boudreaux said. "And this man Charlie Harper."

Patrick glanced up nervously, trying visibly not to look it, then looked back down at his cuff. "Yeah, I heard about Fain," he said, and tried for a sardonic smile. "Ironic, huh?"

Boudreaux placed his palms on his desk, splayed his fingers. "You didn't really think anyone would suspect Maggie Redmond, did you?"

This time, Patrick skipped the smile when he looked at Boudreaux. "I don't really care, actually."

"Tell me about you and Charlie Harper," Boudreaux said, his bright blue eyes hard and steady.

Patrick cut his eyes to the lamp rather than look at Boudreaux. "I don't know him."

"Charlie Harper is the man who shot Maggie Redmond," Boudreaux said.

"Everybody knows that," Patrick said. "It was in the paper."

"At your behest," Boudreaux said.

Patrick flicked at the corner of his mouth with his tongue. "Fain hired him. He likes to make examples of people who steal from him."

"Lie to me again," Boudreaux said quietly.

Patrick knew better than to accept that invitation, but he did it anyway. "I hear Fain hired Harper to kill her."

"They thought Fain killed Graham, too," Boudreaux said.

"Look, Pop. We already went over that," Patrick said. "But I don't have anything to do with Harper."

"When you hire someone to kill a person, because you don't have the guts to do it yourself, you need to avoid contracting imbeciles who think they're on a TV show," Boudreaux said.

"What's that supposed to mean?"

Boudreaux shifted in his chair, and Patrick shrank almost imperceptibly into his beautiful black suit. "It means Harper thought he needed to issue a soundbite before he finished Maggie off."

"What do you mean?" Patrick asked, the corner of his mouth twitching just a bit.

"I mean he said he was 'tired of cleaning up Boudreaux's messes'," Boudreaux answered.

The two men stared at each other for a long moment. It took a good deal of effort on Patrick's part; it was effortless for Boudreaux.

"I don't make messes," Boudreaux said finally. "And if I did, I'd clean them up myself."

Patrick swallowed hard.

"Who killed David Seward? Fain or Charlie Harper?" Boudreaux put his hand up as Patrick opened his mouth. "Be careful. Make certain that anything that comes from your mouth at this moment is true."

Patrick took a moment to answer. "Harper," he said quietly.

"So you steal Fain's drugs, sell them to some other low-life, and then use how much of your profits to kill poor David? Which I can only assume you did so Fain wouldn't get hold of him and find out he didn't steal anything after all."

Boudreaux waited, but Patrick just stared at him. He sighed before speaking again, slowly. "How much did you pay Harper to kill David Seward?"

Patrick chewed the inside of his cheek a moment before answering. "Ten thousand."

"So you shop at Walmart for your assassins," Boudreaux said. He took a breath and let it out slowly. "And how much to kill Maggie Redmond?"

It took Patrick just a bit longer to answer that one. "Ten thousand."

Boudreaux scratched at his left eyebrow for a moment and took a calming breath. "I should think if you were going to defy me, to do something which presented that grave a danger to yourself, that you would have paid much more to someone far more proficient."

Boudreaux watched Patrick's pupils expand, saw him lock his teeth together, saw the vein on the side of his neck pulsating. "I told you, in terms even you could understand, not to go anywhere near Maggie Redmond."

Patrick's left leg started vibrating up and down against the leather armchair, and his face slowly grew pink. Boudreaux thought it was like watching someone get a sunburn through time-lapse photography.

"Well, Pop," Patrick said quietly. "You have my sincerest apology for trying to kill your little girlfriend."

Boudreaux got up slowly from his chair, the creaking of the expensive leather the only sound in the room. Patrick's eyes followed him, blinking rapidly, as he walked to one of the French doors and stood, hands in his pockets, looking out at the yard.

"That comment will go unaddressed, in the interest of continuing this conversation without bloodshed."

He sighed, and gathered his thoughts, and his emotions, as he watched a squirrel sifting through the fallen fruit beneath an avocado tree. "I told you that I was working on something with Maggie. Exactly what that is, is none of your business."

He turned around and regarded Patrick, who tried not to shrink from his gaze.

"So, you going to chop me into little pieces and dump me in the ocean, Pop? Because if you are, I'd like you to get on with it," Patrick said. "Just don't subject me to any of your 'family first' bull while you're doing it."

Boudreaux's eyes narrowed, while Patrick sat there looking like he might jump from the chair at any moment.

"Actually, Patrick, because of that very sentiment, I'm going to accept half the responsibility for your actions."

"What does that mean?"

"It means that I think you've lost your damn mind," Boudreaux said quietly. "I think you've lost it to drugs and greed and bad raising."

"You and Mom raised me," Patrick said.

"Precisely," Boudreaux said. "And failed. Something I've been thinking about quite a bit over the last few weeks."

Patrick's relief must have caused an acute hysteria, for he actually almost laughed. "Are you apologizing to me?" he asked, then instantly seemed to regret it, as Boudreaux slowly walked toward him, his hands still in his pockets.

"Don't be ridiculous. You've fallen too far from grace for me to apologize to you, even for my own mistakes." He stopped a few feet in front of Patrick's chair. "What I am doing is trying to atone, in some small way."

"What way is that?" Patrick asked uncertainly.

"You have one week to get out of the country."

"What?"

"I suggest you go somewhere that doesn't have an extradition agreement with the US," Boudreaux continued. "And make it someplace you can stand to live for the rest of your life, because you won't be coming back."

"I have a career here," Patrick said. "Damn it, I'm the Assistant State's Attorney!"

"You're retiring," Boudreaux said. "You will take whatever money you have left, you will take what is in your trust, and you will get your ass to Venezuela or wherever it is you decide you're going, and you will arrive there no later than one week from today."

Patrick opened and closed his mouth a couple of times before finding his words. "Are you serious?"

"Are you unfamiliar with my serious face, Patrick?" Boudreaux asked quietly.

"I can't just...go into exile and lose everything!"

"Is there something you haven't already lost?"

Patrick didn't answer, just licked his lips nervously.

"One week. I'll release the funds in your trust account when you've arrived where you're going."

"That's not enough to live on indefinitely," Patrick said.

"I suggest you pick someplace with a low cost of living, and develop a marketable skill." Patrick shook his head, his mouth open slightly. "It's time for you to leave this room, Patrick."

Patrick stood up, his hands on the armrests of his chair as though he needed some support. He walked slowly to the door.

"Patrick?" Patrick stopped and turned, his hand on the door knob. "You need to understand that I'm giving you this option because I do feel some responsibility for the man that you've become. I don't want to add you to my already overburdened conscience."

Patrick looked at him a moment, seeming slightly dazed, then walked out of the room and closed the door.

Boudreaux turned around and walked back to the French door. His eyes scanned the yard, but the squirrel was no longer under the avocado tree. His eyes filled suddenly with warmth and moisture, and he pinched at their inner corners, blinked a few times, and stared out at the empty yard.

CHAPTER

TWELVE

aggie breathed in the smell of salt and the slight, metallic odor of rain from tin-colored clouds off to the east. There were few other boats out, and once she checked her coordinates and cut the engine, there was very little sound, outside the slap of the wake against the fiberglass hull.

Maggie dropped the sea anchor, then stretched her back and walked to the port side. She leaned over the rail, hung on with one hand, and just managed to trail the tips of her fingers through the water. When she lifted her hand up, she wondered if any of David's ashes lingered here where they'd spread them, in David's favorite shrimping hole, or they'd all scattered miles away. Still, this was as close as she would get.

She touched her fingers to her neck, and closed her eyes a moment as the sea water cooled her. Then she sat down on one of the bench seats and sighed as she looked out at the water.

She sat there for almost an hour, willing the sun and the water and the sounds of the occasional gull to help her feel grounded again, to remind her of who she was, where she came from, to bring her back to herself.

She stood up and leaned over the rail again, cupped some water and dribbled it over the top of her head, seared by the mid-morning sun. Then she sat back down and sighed.

"So, I hope you realize that you left me with almost nobody to talk to," she said quietly. "Not like us, anyway."

She looked up as a couple of gulls flew overhead, arguing about something pertinent to gulls, then she looked back out at the water.

"I'm not sure how much you still care about what goes on around here, but I gave Sky your truck. I see her sometimes when she's leaving or getting home, and she sits in it for an extra minute or two. Kyle has your guitar, the new one, and he's gone back to practicing almost every day."

Maggie chewed at the corner of her lip, as she watched the two gulls dive, then take back off, one of them with a small fish in its beak.

"Wyatt's angry with me," she said finally. "I may even have...I don't know, I think maybe that's not fixable. I would never have asked your advice about it, but I bet you would have given me some if I did."

Maggie blinked back tears as she got a scent memory of sun-warmed flannel and Jovan Musk. "Or maybe...maybe I would have just forgotten about Wyatt, because how good is a man who would give that kind of advice to his ex-wife?"

She laughed softly, but she had to blink a few more times. "You know, I keep wondering if they have baseball in Heaven, because every time I picture you there, you're taking practice swings. Or rounding second base."

She suddenly felt a little self-conscious, and looked down at her hands. "Anyway," she said. She picked at a hangnail on the middle finger of her right hand. "You know I loved you, right?"

⚓ ⚓ ⚓

Wyatt stood with his hands on his hips near one of the stainless-steel tables, watching Deputy Mike Calder scrape the inside of the last drain.

Calder had already done the other nine floor drains, as well as swabbed the rims, inspected for hairs, and collected swabs from the grout between the white, square-foot tiles.

Judge Richardson, one of the few judges that Wyatt suspected might grant him the search warrant, had allowed for Wyatt, one deputy trained in biological evidence collection, and one other deputy, mainly for appearances. He had not agreed to a forensic team from Tallahassee.

When Wyatt had first shown Boudreaux the search warrant, Boudreaux had called his attorney, who had immediately conveyed to the court that the use of Luminol, to detect blood trace in a room used to process food, presented a danger to the public. Wyatt thought it funny, even in his present frame of mind, that the new search warrant, with that addendum, had been faxed to Boudreaux's office. Wyatt wasn't too bent out of shape about the Luminol. Blood ran all over the floor all day long. The whole damn room would probably light up, without giving them anything they didn't already know.

Across the long, narrow room, Bennett Boudreaux leaned against the wall by the walk-in coolers, arms folded loosely across his chest. He was put out, but had been polite and decidedly unconcerned when Wyatt, Mike and Deputy Gina Farrell had shown up with the search warrant. The receptionist had seemed far more upset by it than

Boudreaux had, but she looked like the type to get easily upset. Boudreaux was not.

Boudreaux had sent the dozen or so fish processors out on an extended break, sent the receptionist fluttering back down the hallway, and been watching Wyatt and his team from the wall since that time, almost two hours.

Wyatt saw Boudreaux looking at his expensive watch, and he wandered over there, more out of a need to stretch his legs than anything else.

"How much longer do you think you'll need, Sheriff Hamilton?" Boudreaux asked as Wyatt approached him.

Wyatt put his hands on his hips and glanced over at Mike, who was putting the drain cover back into place. "Not much longer," he answered with a shrug.

"I'm not trying to be difficult," Boudreaux said. "We just have a lot of fish waiting to be dressed yet today."

"I understand," Wyatt said politely.

Boudreaux nodded his head toward Mike and Deputy Farrell. "I'm surprised this is all you brought with you," he said.

"This is all I was allowed," Wyatt said.

"You have a law enforcement officer stating that she's certain I killed Sport Wilmette, and all you got was Deputy Dan with his Q-tips?"

"That's your way of asking me if I do have a law enforcement officer who said any such thing. I won't be responding to that question."

"For the record, she told you with my blessing."

"I'm sure she appreciated that," Wyatt said. "For the record, what I *have* is a witness who saw you let Wilmette in that Tuesday night, then saw you leave, but never saw Wilmette come out." He looked over at Boudreaux. "And a confidential informant who says that Wilmette might have been trying to blackmail you."

Boudreaux knew damn well there was no confidential informant. The only one who knew about Wilmette's attempt to get money from him was Maggie. He held Wyatt's gaze for a moment. "You didn't tell them about Maggie," he said, his surprise cool but evident.

Wyatt didn't answer, just leaned back against the wall and watched as Mike and Deputy Farrell started putting things back into Mike's case.

"Well, given that circumstance, I'm surprised you got a search warrant at all," Boudreaux said.

"Judge Richardson's not that fond of you."

"I'm aware of that, yes," Boudreaux said pleasantly.

Wyatt checked his watch without unfolding his arms from his chest.

"Why *didn't* you say anything about Maggie?" Boudreaux asked.

Wyatt just looked at him, then looked away.

"We both know what we're talking about here, so I don't see why you're hesitant to explain that to me."

Wyatt looked at him, his brows knit together. "Look. I realize you and Maggie have some kind of semi-confessional *pas de deux* going on, but you and I don't have that kind of relationship."

"I can understand why that bothers you," Boudreaux said

"What? That you and I aren't real close?"

One corner of Boudreaux's mouth curled up in something that threatened to be a smile. Then he and Wyatt both watched as the other two officers crossed the room.

"I can understand it troubling you, given your own relationship," Boudreaux said. Wyatt turned and looked at him. "You *are* her supervisor."

"I'm all set, boss," Mike said as he and Deputy Farrell approached.

"All right," Wyatt said, pushing off from the wall.

Mike and Farrell preceded him the few feet to the door, and Farrell opened it. Wyatt watched them both go out into the hall, then turned to look at Boudreaux.

"I'm concerned because I'm responsible for her," Wyatt said.

Boudreaux nodded. "Yes, you are. I hope you don't forget that."

Wyatt looked at him a moment, then opened the door and walked out.

⚓ ⚓ ⚓

Maggie had just crossed the parking lot at the marina, heading back to her Jeep, when she saw Wyatt's car and another cruiser parked in front of Sea-Fair, next door. She changed direction and walked that way. She was halfway across the Sea-Fair parking lot, oyster shells crunching beneath her hiking boots, when Mike Calder and Gina Farrell walked out the front door. Wyatt was right behind them.

Maggie stopped, noted the crime scene case in Mike's hand. He saw her and waved, and she raised a hand back, including Gina in the gesture. She looked away from them as they turned toward the cruiser. Wyatt was standing in the middle of the lot, hands on his hips, staring at her.

She stared back for a moment, then started over to him. "What's going on?" she asked when she was a few feet away.

Wyatt gave her a look that clearly indicated she'd asked a ridiculous question.

"Did you find anything?" she asked.

As she reached him, he took her elbow and started walking her the way she'd just come. "If I had, I wouldn't be able to discuss it with you, would I?"

"I'm just asking," she said.

"I'm just not answering," he said, though his tone wasn't especially unkind. "What are you doing here? You and Boudreaux don't have a lunch date, do you?"

"No, smartass, I just came back in Daddy's boat," she said.

"Where were you?"

"I took a mental health break out on the water," she said, stepping over a sparsely planted median between the two parking lots.

"How's your mental health?" he asked.

"About what you'd expect. How's yours?"

"Not as vigorous as it was before I moved here," he answered. They stopped at her Jeep, and he let go of her elbow.

"Wyatt, I'm sorry," Maggie said. "Last night—"

He nodded, almost dismissively. "We were both upset. Listen, I need you to stay away from Boudreaux. I need you to stay away from that whole damn family, you understand?"

"What's going on?"

"No, not questions, just compliance. Can you give being compliant a shot? Cause that would make my life quite a bit easier right now."

Maggie stood up a little straighter, the literal manifestation of getting her back up. "Yeah, I can comply."

"Thank you," he said.

"Can you at least tell me what you think?"

He jammed his hands onto his hips. "About what?"

Maggie sighed. "About Boudreaux."

Wyatt pulled off his ball cap and slapped it back on. "Oh, I can talk to you all damn day and half the night about what I think about Boudreaux," he said. "I think he was wholly unconcerned about me coming in there with a search warrant, because he's careful as hell. We swabbed all over that tile floor, but we're not going to find anything, Maggie. I can almost bet on that."

Maggie folded her arms across her chest. "Okay," she said.

"I also think that he's definitely got a thing of some kind for you, and that this doesn't necessarily make you any safer with him," Wyatt said. "For all we know, his last sixteen girlfriends all went into the ocean, too."

"Has he had sixteen girlfriends?"

"Well, how the hell would I know? But you're right, he does have significant charm, which I think I dislike quite a bit."

"I've never heard of any girlfriends, dead or otherwise," Maggie said.

Wyatt raised an eyebrow. "Have you met his wife?"

"Barely," Maggie said, her distaste evident.

"She's a real piece of work," Wyatt said. "I'm surprised she's lived this long. Of course, he's Roman Catholic, so maybe he thinks she's his penance."

Maggie shrugged and Wyatt looked away for a moment, watched a date palm dance a little in the slight breeze, and then looked back at her. "My point is that I think his interest in you is a lot more personal than I originally thought, and that's not necessarily a good thing."

"Why do you think that?"

"Because I have a prostate," he said. She squinted her eyes at him and he elaborated. "I'm a man."

"Well, I'm a woman and I think you're off base. I would know if he was interested in that way."

"Really? When did you know I was interested, Maggie?"

She looked away from him for a second and shrugged a little. "When you told me."

"Bingo. Did you know Dudley Do-Right had it bad for you right up until he got married?"

"Dwight? No he didn't!"

"How about Axel Blackwell, did you know about that?"

"Wyatt, Axel was David's closest friend. I've known him since we were like twelve."

"Case rested." Wyatt said. "You don't have a clue about men where you're concerned."

"I'm sorry, Wyatt, but I don't get that vibe from Boudreaux at all."

"You don't get vibes, period." He took his cap off again and ran a hand through his damp hair. "Would you just please do what I ask and stay away from the guy?"

"Okay," Maggie answered.

"Thank you. Now, I need to go to the courthouse." He put his cap back on. "I'll see you at work."

"Okay," Maggie said quietly. She watched him walk back over to the Sea-Fair parking lot, a sadness weighing in her chest for just a moment, before she pushed it down, compartmentalized it, as was her habit. Then she got in her Jeep.

She sat there for a moment with the door open. The interior of the Jeep was like a rice cooker, and she was damp from the trapped humidity the moment she got in. She started the engine and turned the air on with the door still open, and watched Wyatt pull out onto Water Street and make a left.

She tried to push her worries about Wyatt out of her mind by focusing on something that had bugged her when he'd been talking about Boudreaux, but it wouldn't come back to her. She gave up when the inside of the car become bearable enough to close the door and leave.

THIRTEEN

She pulled out onto Water Street and made a left, as Wyatt had. The niggling came back to her as she waited at Apalach's token red light, but was gone by the time she made a right to head over to her parents.

On impulse, she pulled into Piggly-Wiggly a few blocks later. She knew the sudden decision to pick up a bottle of wine was probably just a way of delaying the conversation she knew she was about to have, but she figured they'd probably need the wine anyway.

She was coming back out with a bottle of Riesling she didn't remember actually choosing, when she saw John Solomon headed toward the door. John had been with the Sheriff's Office for twenty years, then took a job as the director of the Chamber of Commerce, where he seemed to have found his real calling.

He seemed to really enjoy working on things like the Florida Seafood Festival, the biggest in the state, and the town's celebration in Riverfront Park on the 3rd of July. It had been there that David had been killed, his boat blown up as he headed out for a night of shrimping. John had been a hero that night, jumping into the river to help rescue one of David's crewmen.

He smiled at her as they met each other in the parking lot. "Hey, Maggie, how are you?"

"I'm good, John, how are you?"

"Pretty good, pretty good. Hotter than heck." He frowned at her. "Maggie, I know I said it before, but I am so genuinely sorry about David."

"I know. Thank you."

"Man, it just seems like there's way too much tragedy going on this summer," he said. "First David, now those poor people from—was it Nicaragua?"

"Guatemala."

"Right. Just an awful thing. Especially those kids." He looked down for a second. "What's gonna happen to 'em?"

Maggie shook her head. "I don't know. The guy from Homeland Security says Guatemala won't take the bodies back."

"What? So what are we supposed to do, put 'em back?"

"I don't know. I'm kind of out of the loop."

"That's nuts. They've got to have people back home that'll want to bury 'em, get some closure."

Maggie nodded. "Yeah. But we don't even know who most of them are."

John sighed and they were silent for a moment.

"Well, I've got to run, John," Maggie said. "It was good to see you, though."

"Yeah. Yeah sure. Me, too. Margo just wanted me to pick up some floor cleaner. New puppy." He patted her on the shoulder. "You and the kids take care, huh? Call me if I can do anything."

"I will." Maggie lifted a hand at him, and she watched him as he started for the store, his eyes on the ground until he got to the door. Then she walked to the Jeep and got in.

She had just started the engine when the niggling that wouldn't go away came back, with clarity. The floor. Wyatt said they'd swabbed the tile floor at Sea-Fair. But when she'd been in the new processing room to talk to Boudreaux about Wilmette, the floor had been bare concrete.

Maggie pulled her cell out of her purse and dialed Wyatt. It went straight to voice mail. She left him a message to call her, then took a deep breath and headed for her parents'.

⚓ ⚓ ⚓

Wyatt walked out of Judge Richardson's reception area and down the granite, second-floor hallway of the courthouse. As he walked, he tucked his copies of the folded paperwork into his small leather binder. When he looked back up, he saw Patrick Boudreaux standing by the stairs, thumbing a message on his phone.

A wave of heat he could almost see as being red coursed upwards from his stomach to his chest, and he breathed in slowly through his nose, then exhaled through his mouth. He tapped the binder against his thigh as he approached Patrick, then stopped.

"Hello, Patrick," he said politely.

When Patrick looked up, the hint of distaste on his face almost distracted from the shadows under his eyes, which Wyatt was surprised he hadn't called in sick for.

"Sheriff Hamilton. You here for another search warrant for my father?" he asked, working up half a smirk.

"No, I'm here on other business," Wyatt said pleasantly.

"Your own, I hope," Patrick said, and looked back down at his phone.

Wyatt smiled and walked around Patrick to the head of the stairs. He started down, then stopped and looked back at Patrick. "Are you gay?"

Patrick looked up quickly, his lip curling. "No, I'm not *gay*," he said.

"Huh," Wyatt said. "You might want to try harder. It might make your prospects more agreeable."

"I'll pretend I didn't hear that," Patrick said, his face reddening.

"Well, while you're at it, you can pretend you understood it," Wyatt said, and headed down the stairs.

⚓ ⚓ ⚓

Maggie's parents were sitting at the table on the back deck when she walked out there with the bottle of wine and three glasses. Kyle and Sky were sitting on the steps, watching something on Sky's phone.

"Hey, y'all," Maggie said.

"Hey, Sunshine," Gray said.

Georgia put out a hand and brushed Maggie's arm as she set the glasses down on the table. "Hey, sweetie. Long day?"

"Yeah, kind of," Maggie said. She set the bottle down in front of Gray. "Can you open that, Daddy?"

"Is it a cork?"

"No. But my hand, I still have a little trouble with it."

"I thought Dr. Vinson said it would be fine," Georgia said.

"It will," Maggie said. "It's just the nerve. I have trouble with squeezing little things."

Gray started opening the wine, and Maggie walked over and kissed each of her kids on the top of the head. "Hey, guys."

"Hey, Mom," Kyle said without looking up.

"Hey," Sky said.

Maggie looked at Sky's phone. They were watching a YouTube video of a skinny, young black man dancing.

"What's that?" she asked.

"Some guy breakdancing," Kyle said.

"It's dubstep, dork," Sky said.

"Whatever."

"What's dubstep?" Gray asked as Maggie sat down at the table.

"I don't know," she answered. "I think maybe we used to call it Techno."

"Do I know what Techno is?" he asked, pouring their wine.

"Probably not," she said.

"Good," he answered.

"Honey, we're going to grill some fish later," Georgia said. "Do you guys want to stay and eat?"

"Um, you know what, Mom? I don't know," Maggie answered. She took a swallow of the wine.

"So what's this thing you need to talk to us about?" Gray asked. Maggie looked over at the kids. "Is it something we need to send the kids inside for?"

"No. No, I need them to listen, too."

"Is it something about David?" Georgia asked.

Maggie looked over at the steps as Kyle looked over his shoulder at her. "No, Mom."

"Is it something with work?"

"Georgia, honey, we'll know what it's about when she tells it," Gray said.

Maggie waved Kyle over. "You guys, can you come over here for a minute?"

Georgia took a decent swallow of her wine as the kids got up and walked over to the table. Sky was texting as she sat down.

"Sky, I need you to stay off the phone for a minute, okay?"

"Okay, hold up," Sky said without looking at her.

Kyle took a drink from a can of RC that sat on the table in front of him. "What's going on?"

Maggie looked at Sky, who glanced up at her, tapped her phone, and set it down on the table. "Sorry." She leaned back. "So what's up?"

Maggie took a breath and looked at Kyle. "First, I need to know, Kyle, do you know what rape is?"

Kyle swallowed. "Yeah."

"Are you sure?"

"Yeah. But, like, you're not gonna make me prove it are you?"

"No."

"He knows, Mom. Serious," Sky said. "Dude, there's not like a serial rapist running around or something is there?"

"No, not at the moment," Maggie said.

"What's going on, baby?" Gray asked quietly.

Maggie took a deep breath and let it out, then looked at each of her parents, settling on her mother. "Do you guys remember when I was fifteen, I fell off my bike, banged myself up pretty good?"

Georgie frowned a minute, then shook her head. "No, I don't remember that."

Maggie looked at her Dad, and he shook his head. "I don't think I do, honey."

"Was this in town?" Georgia asked.

"No. I was fishing, down Bluff Road. You know, the woods by that sandy spot on the river. It was in November, right before Thanksgiving."

Gray sat forward slowly, leaned on the table. "I remember it," he said quietly. He looked at Maggie. "You hurt your back."

Maggie nodded. "Yeah. I did." She glanced over at the kids and her Mom, but then looked back at Gray when she spoke. "But I didn't fall off my bike. I was raped."

Georgia gasped, but no one else spoke for a moment. Maggie watched as Gray tried to keep his face from collapsing. He laid his hands out flat on the table and rested them there. Finally, Georgia reached over and put her hand on her daughter's.

"Baby, why didn't you tell us?" she asked gently.

"I'm sorry, Mom. I couldn't. I didn't."

"Mom?" Sky asked. "Are you okay?"

"Sky baby, it was a long time ago."

Sky's eyes watered. "I'm really sorry."

Kyle shifted in his chair. "But, you were younger than Sky."

Maggie nodded. "Yeah, buddy. I was."

Kyle looked down, focused on scraping a thumbnail against the soda can.

"Who did this, Maggie?" Gray stared at the table as he spoke. "Was this a stranger?"

"No. I mean, I didn't know him, but I knew who he was."

Gray looked up at her and waited.

"It was Gregory Boudreaux," she said quietly.

"The guy that shot himself last month?" Sky asked.

Maggie nodded at her daughter. "Yes."

"Good," Kyle said to his soda can.

Georgia coughed softly and Maggie looked over at her. Her eyes were large as she looked back at Maggie. "Excuse me. I'm sorry," she said, as she got up.

They watched her walk through the open sliding glass door, then Maggie looked back at her Dad. After a moment, he looked back at her. "Gregory Boudreaux."

"Yes."

Gray nodded slowly, then took a swallow of his wine, stared at the glass after he set it back down.

"Mom?" Sky asked. Maggie looked at her. "He did kill himself, right?"

"Yeah, Sky." Maggie put a hand on hers. "Yeah."

Sky nodded. "I mean, I wouldn't blame you. I'm sorry."

Maggie shook her head. "It's okay."

She looked at Gray, who was still staring into his wine, then she looked over at the door. "I'm going to go check on Mom," she said as she got up.

She heard the toilet flush as she walked down the short hallway off of the living room, then heard the water running. When she opened the bathroom door, her mother was rinsing her mouth in the sink.

She stood up and looked at Maggie in the mirror. "I'm sorry, honey. I just—the shock."

"Are you okay, Mom?"

"Am I okay? Maggie. Who cares if I'm okay?"

"I'm sorry," Maggie said.

Georgia turned around and grabbed up Maggie's hands. "I can't help thinking I should have sensed it. I'm your mother—I'm a *woman*, and I didn't even sense it."

"Mom, how many times have you told me how good I am at shutting people out?"

Georgia dropped one of Maggie's hands and put her hand to her chest. "Only since you were a teenager."

Maggie shrugged a little. "Yeah."

"It's getting too close in here," Georgia said, fanning her chest with her hand.

Maggie stepped back out of the bathroom, and her mother brushed past her. Maggie followed her into the kitchen, watched her mother as she opened the fridge and took out a tray of fish filets.

Maggie stood there for a few moments, as her mother pulled a grill rack out of the oven drawer, grabbed some salt and seasonings from a cupboard, and a lemon from a bowl on the counter. Every now and then, Georgia looked Maggie's way, but never met her eyes.

"I'm sorry," Georgia finally said. "I just need something to do with my hands. I just need to process this for a minute. I need to pray, is what I need to do."

"It's okay, Mom. I'm going to go back outside, okay?"

"Okay," Georgia said to the fish.

Maggie walked back out to the deck. The kids were sitting where she'd left them, but Gray was standing, leaning against the stair rail. Maggie put a hand on Kyle's shoulder.

"You guys, why don't you go inside and get your stuff together and we'll head home in a minute, okay? I just want to talk to Granddad for a little bit."

They both stood up, and Kyle walked inside. Sky put an arm around her mother's neck for a moment, and Maggie patted her back. Then Sky followed Kyle into the house.

Maggie walked over to the stairs, and Gray put his hands in his pockets, walked down the steps. Maggie followed him, and they walked slowly across the grass toward the dock.

"Mom's hurt because I didn't tell her," Maggie said after a minute.

"Your mama's hurt because she can't undo it," he said.

Maggie looked over at him as they walked. He was looking down at the grass, at his old Docksiders as they whispered through it. A longish lock of his sandy brown hair fell over his widow's peak, over one eye, and he ignored it. Maggie could see his jaw working as he thought.

"I can understand why you didn't tell me," he said, not looking at her. "A young girl...that would be a hard thing to tell a man, even your daddy."

"Daddy, I wasn't ashamed."

"You damn well better not have been."

"But you would have killed him, and then where would I be?"

He stopped, and she stopped with him. When he looked at her, she thought his green eyes had lost some of their color. She wanted to put it back. "Daddy, I'm really—"

"Don't apologize to me, Margaret Anne. I don't think I could stand it," he said quietly. Maggie swallowed and looked away toward the bay. "Talk to me about Bennett Boudreaux," Gray said.

"What about him?" she asked.

"I can count on one hand the number of times I've ever heard you mention his name," he said. "But Gregory Boudreaux kills himself and suddenly you're sitting at Boss Oyster with the man, and dancing with him at the Cajun Festival. Talk to me about that."

"Well, I mean, I was working his nephew's case," Maggie said. "But then, I don't know. He fascinates me, I guess. And I wondered what he wanted."

"What he wanted," Gray repeated. "What does he want?"

"Atonement, maybe?"

Gray squinted at her a moment. "He knew about this?"

"Gregory told him the night before he killed himself."

"He told you this?"

"Yes."

Gray looked off toward the water, his eyes flicking back and forth as he worked things in his mind. "What else is going on? You're telling us now for a reason."

Maggie sighed. "Oh, Daddy. What a damn mess." Gray watched her and waited. "Brandon Wilmette, the guy with the foot?" Gray nodded. "He was trying to blackmail Boudreaux about the rape. He thought Boudreaux would want to save himself the embarrassment."

"And how did this man know about it?"

"He was there. I never saw him, but I knew he was there. He was watching."

Her chest seemed to knot together as she watched her father's face. New lines and cracks seemed to form before her eyes, and his face seemed to disassemble and reassemble within seconds, as though an audience for her rape was worse than the thing itself.

After a moment, he let out a slow breath and looked back out at the bay, then he looked at Maggie. "I'm assuming you're telling me he killed him."

"Yes." She swallowed. "Wyatt executed a search warrant at Sea-Fair today."

"You told Wyatt."

"I had to. I had no business on these cases," she said. "And I was tired of the secrets." Gray nodded. "But if they arrest Boudreaux, it'll come out. I needed you and the kids to already know."

"There's all kinds of nasty things about Boudreaux that are public knowledge or at least public rumor," Gray said. "He didn't kill that man because he was afraid of being embarrassed."

"No."

He looked at her for a moment, long enough for her to wonder if he was waiting for her to say something. "Did he tell you why he did it?"

"I think he thought it was the right thing to do," Maggie said. "I know that sounds crazy."

"No, it sounds about right. For him." Maggie tilted her head at him. "I sold the man oysters for forty years, Maggie. We're not strangers."

Maggie nodded, and they both looked elsewhere for a moment.

"You know, Maggie, I didn't remember that day, the thing with the bike," Gray said finally. "But you did change around that time, and I did notice. For a long time, I thought it was David's fault."

"What do you mean?"

"I thought maybe you'd lost your virginity." He huffed a small laugh, but there was no humor in it. "That's awful young for a girl, and I thought it had made you different, made you keep more to yourself."

"No wonder you were so hard on us back then," she said. "Every time we turned around, there you were, and David was actually intimidated by you. That was weird for him; you guys were so close. David and I never—we didn't do anything really, until we were married."

Gray nodded. "Yeah. I figured that out after a while." He looked at her, almost apologetically. "I figured it was just teenage girl stuff."

Maggie nodded.

"Maggie, I'd really like it if you stayed away from Boudreaux," Gray said.

"Yeah. You and Wyatt both."

"I bet that's true," he said. "Nobody's all bad, any more than anyone is all good, Maggie. But I think he's bad for *you*."

Maggie nodded and looked back at the house. "I need to take the kids home, talk to them," she said. "I'm sorry, but I can't really talk to Mom about it anymore right now."

"Don't worry about your mama," he said. "She's strong stuff. Stronger than I am. She's not like us, though; she lets it all out for a bit, and then she bucks up. You and I, we just buck up and wait for somebody to drag it out of us."

"Yeah." Maggie tried to smile. "That we do."

CHAPTER

FOURTEEN

K yle opted to ride home with Maggie, while Sky followed in David's truck.

Clouds were heading in from the east, and the breeze had picked up a bit in anticipation of a cooling rain. Maggie rolled the windows down, and breathed deeply.

Kyle was quiet until they were out of town, heading up Bluff Road. "I would never do that to a girl," he said finally, staring out the windshield.

Maggie looked over at him, and he looked back at her, looking so much like David that she felt like she was looking at a memory. It occurred to her then that Kyle was now the same age David had been when they'd first met.

"I know," she said. "He was sick, Kyle."

"I don't really care," he said.

"Me, neither."

He looked back out at the road.

"I'm glad he's dead," he said quietly.

"Me, too."

⚓ ⚓ ⚓

When they got home, they calmed Stoopid, who had a great deal of information to share, and soothed Coco, who had missed her kids profoundly.

Uncharacteristically, Sky opted to hang out in the kitchen with Maggie while she cooked dinner. They worked in silence for some time, Maggie cutting vegetables for roasting while Sky, unasked, put the dishes away. Then she leaned up against the counter and watched her mother.

"Were you really scared?" she asked finally.

Maggie looked up from the cutting board. "Yeah," she said casually. "Sure. But it was a long time ago."

Sky was quiet again for a moment as she watched Maggie spread the vegetables on a baking sheet and toss them with some oil.

"Mom?" Sky ran her finger around in a drop of oil that had splattered onto the tile counter. "I'm really sorry about all the times I called you a paranoid freak."

Maggie laughed. "It's okay. I just worry about you. I would have anyway."

"Sure, dude," Sky said, trying to smile. "I'd have known how to handle a Mossberg by the age of twelve anyway."

"Yeah, you probably would have, dude," Maggie said. "There are guns here. You guys need to know how and when to handle them. Period."

Sky smiled at her, and Maggie put some salt and pepper on the vegetables before putting them in the oven. When she straightened up, Sky was watching her.

"What?" she asked her.

Sky shrugged a little. "I'm proud of you."

Maggie felt a warmth in her stomach. "For what?"

"Just, for being okay, I guess," she said.

Maggie smiled at her. "I am."

"I don't feel right about leaving you alone tonight."

Sky had a group date planned, and Kyle was invited to a birthday sleepover.

"Baby, I've been alone here plenty of times, remember?"

"Yeah, but it just doesn't seem right. You know, tonight."

Maggie shook her head. "It's fine. Caroline and Brian are leaving for college soon. You should spend time with them."

"I can come back early," Sky said.

"Said Sky never," said Maggie, laughing. "It's fine, Sky. I promise."

Maggie took the cutting board to the sink and started washing it. Her heart almost stopped when Sky's arms slid around her and she felt Sky's head on her back. Hugs had been few and far between the last few years.

"I love you, homes," Sky said quietly.

Maggie blinked back tears and smiled. "I love you, too, dawg."

$$\text{⚓ ⚓ ⚓}$$

Maggie turned onto Seventh Street and looked over at Kyle. "Did you remember your phone charger?" she asked him.

"Yeah, I got it," he said.

"I'm off tomorrow, so call me when everybody's getting ready to leave so I can come get you," she said.

"I will. But it's probably not gonna be til like four or five, Josh said."

"That's fine." Maggie rubbed at her right eye. She hadn't changed her contacts in days and her eyes felt like they had sand in them. She just wanted to go home and go to bed.

"Unless his little brothers go all bat—get nuts again, then we're all gonna scatter," he said.

Maggie looked at him, one eyebrow raised. "You need to hang out with your sister less."

"You told us we needed to hang out more," he said, deadpan.

Maggie was coming up with a reply when her cell rang. Kyle picked it up from the console. "It's Wyatt," he said.

"Oh, give it to me," she said, as she stopped at a stop sign.

She thumbed the answer button. "Hey," she said.

"Hey. What are you doing?" he asked.

"Dropping Kyle off for a sleepover."

"Oh. Well, I wondered if maybe you wanted to come by here."

"Are you at home?"

"Yeah."

"Did you get my message?" she asked.

"Yeah. You can tell me whatever that is when you get here, but that's not why I'm asking."

"Oh. Okay, well, I'll be there in a few minutes."

"Okay."

"Okay," she echoed dumbly, then hung up.

Kyle was looking at her. "What?" she asked.

"It's a stop sign, not a train," he said, rolling his eyes.

"Shut up, Kyle," she said, smiling. She started driving again. "You really need to stop hanging out with Sky."

Kyle grinned at her. "So, you're going over to Wyatt's?"

"Yeah."

"Tell him I'm almost done with his book."

"Which book?"

"He's getting me into James Lee Burke."

Maggie looked over at him as she pulled into Josh's driveway. "Really. You're kind of young for his books."

"I'm ten."

"Yeah."

Kyle grabbed his backpack out of the back seat. "Well, I can go back to Goosebumps if you want, but Dave Robicheaux is better for my vocabulary."

He plopped the backpack on his lap and looked at her. "Dad liked suspense stuff, too," he said, more subdued.

Maggie's chest tickled just a bit. "Yeah. He did."

"Okay, well." Kyle gave her half a smile. "Hopefully, this'll be better than last year."

She smiled and ruffled his soft, black hair. "Have fun, buddy."

"I will." He leaned over and got a hug, then opened the door. "See ya later."

Maggie watched him go to the door, waved at Josh's mom Shelly, then backed out of the driveway.

⚓   ⚓   ⚓

Patrick put his rocks glass of tequila down next to the gun on the glass and marble coffee table, and waited for the burning in his throat to subside. Then he picked up the little glass vial, unscrewed the cap with the little gold spoon built into it, got a tiny scoop, and stuck the spoon under his right nostril.

He snorted the coke, sniffed a couple of times, then licked a finger and dabbed at the residue on the spoon, rubbed it on his upper gum. He closed the vial again and set it down and picked up his drink, dripping condensation onto the marled grip of the gun.

The Smith & Wesson Model 67-1 Revolver 38 Special. The first gun Pop had ever given him, when he was fourteen. It had come complete with a spiel about how "special" it was, and Patrick had thought it was exceptionally cool-looking, with all that stainless steel, so shiny and new. Unfortunately, in order to keep the cool-looking gun, he actually had to spend several hours out in the blistering sun with Pop, learning how to use it.

He thought it all very symbolic, kind of like with Fain, but this symbolism was for him alone. He wondered if Pop would appreciate it, then admitted to himself that he wasn't going to give Pop time to appreciate anything. He might be a fool, but he wasn't stupid.

No, he wasn't going to give the old man any speeches or ask him to appreciate any irony. It was going to be straight to business, because Pop was slick and Pop was fast, and the real irony would be if Patrick was the only one who didn't live through the night. No fooling around with the old man.

The cold, calculating, superior hard-ass.

Patrick downed the rest of the tequila in one go, wincing as it burned first his throat and then his chest. It was the good stuff, the Copas Anejo in the limited edition bottle with the glass cork. Might as well.

He stood up, and only then realized that he'd had a little more tequila than he'd thought. He snatched up his vial, snorted another two spoons, and waited there a moment until he felt some clarity and fire come back to him. Then he dropped the vial into his suit blazer pocket and headed for the door.

He was halfway across the room before he stopped and turned back, a giggle escaping from his throat.

He'd almost forgotten his gun, damn it, and that just would have sucked so much.

CHAPTER

FIFTEEN

Wyatt's rented cottage was a block from Lafayette Park, where Maggie and Boudreaux had walked out onto the pier. If she drove on another five blocks and hung a left, she would be at Boudreaux's house. She wondered, as she pulled into Wyatt's driveway, if Boudreaux still respected her decision to tell Wyatt the truth. She also wondered if it was actually respect he felt, or just confidence in his own proper planning.

Wyatt's front door was open and the lights were on. She could see into the house through the screen door, but she didn't see Wyatt.

She got out and walked to the front porch through an atypically light rain, and tapped on the aluminum frame of the screen door. A moment later, Wyatt appeared from the kitchen area. She watched him walk across the living room. He was barefoot, wearing loose cargo pants and a green denim shirt with the tails hanging.

"Hey," he said as he opened the screen door for her.

"Hey."

Wyatt stepped back and let her in. "Sorry, it's kinda warm in here. My AC's crapped out."

He closed the screen door behind Maggie, and she got a whiff of soap and denim. She hugged her purse a little closer to her hip, unsure what to do at the point at which they ordinarily might have hugged hello.

He looked down at her, and he didn't really seem to know what to do, either. "You want a glass of wine?"

"Sure."

She followed him into the kitchen, separated from the living room by a half wall that turned into a hallway to the bedrooms. Wyatt walked behind the tiled breakfast bar between the kitchen and the eating area, opened the fridge, and took out a bottle of white wine.

Maggie looked toward the open French doors that made up the back wall of the dining area. They led out to the back patio where she and Wyatt had had their first date. The floor-length white sheer curtains ruffled a bit in the breeze, and she heard the rain gently tapping on the patio. She looked away from the doors and set her purse down on the floor and climbed up onto one of the stools as Wyatt set two glasses of wine on the breakfast bar.

"So what's up?" she asked after she took a sip.

"You first. Let's get the work stuff out of the way first."

"What?"

"Your message," he said.

"Oh. Yeah. You said the floor...in the processing room, you said it was tile."

Wyatt took a swallow of his wine. "Yeah, why?"

"It wasn't tile when I was there. It was just concrete."

Wyatt looked at her. "Great," he said, sighing. "Okay. I'll go back to Richardson in the morning."

"Tomorrow's Saturday."

"Okay, Monday. Whatever. Boudreaux's not going to pull up the concrete." They looked at each other a moment and Wyatt sighed. "Lily died because she had the lumpectomy."

Maggie blinked a few times. Wyatt looked down at his wine. "They did the chemo and the radiation, but by the time she decided to have the mastectomy after all, it had spread to her right lung and her bones. She was dead eight months later."

"I'm sorry, Wyatt."

"Me, too." He took another drink of his wine. "But I may have let that color my reaction to you a little bit."

Maggie sighed and shook her head. "No. It was wrong and I knew it was wrong." She looked up at him. "I wanted to talk to you about it. I just didn't know how for some reason. And then it just...snowballed."

Wyatt nodded at her, and she looked out at the patio, tried to blink some moisture back into her tired, scratchy eyes.

"I told them earlier," she said.

"Told who what?"

Maggie chewed the corner of her lip and watched the curtains flutter. "I told my parents and the kids about what happened to me."

Wyatt was quiet for a moment. "Maggie." She looked over at him. "I didn't say anything about it.

Maggie stopped breathing for a moment, and had a fleeting thought that she'd like to go back in time a few hours.

Wyatt sighed. "I got the search warrant without it. Maybe not as good a search warrant, but I got one."

Maggie looked down at the breakfast bar, at the grout between the small ceramic tiles.

"I'm sorry," Wyatt said. "I should have told you that at Boudreaux's, but I had a lot going on in my head. Geez." He rubbed a palm over his face. "I'm sorry."

Maggie stared at the bar for a moment, then she thought about Sky putting her arms around her at the sink and telling her she was proud of her. She shook her head. "No. No, it worked out the way it should. It was time."

⚓ ⚓ ⚓

Patrick took a little extra time at the stop sign to check his nose and his teeth, then almost hit an old man and his little dog when he let off the brake before seeing they were crossing the street. He scowled back at the old man, even though he knew he wouldn't see it through the tinted glass, then shook his head and drove on. Some people were too old even to cross the road properly.

He'd considered using a Sharpie to write *Open Here* on his chest before heading over to the old homeplace, and he'd laughed as he'd thought about the old ME, Larry Davenport, cutting away his shirt sometime tomorrow. Maybe the old bird would finally drop dead of a heart attack. In the end, though, Patrick hadn't been up to writing upside down and backwards, so he'd buttoned back up and said screw it.

It occurred to him, as he accidentally cruised through the next stop sign, that after tomorrow, people were going to start looking at poor Craig a little differently, waiting for the last Boudreaux standing to blow his head off, too. He felt kind of bad about that for a second, then he remembered that he didn't actually like his little brother all that much.

He slowed down as he approached the next corner, and his heart pounded in a more noticeable fashion. He cut his eyes to the right as he approached the house two houses from the corner. When he saw the black car in the driveway, he could actually taste bile rising up in his throat. He paused appropriately at the stop sign, then pulled around the corner and stopped.

Then he looked around him at the empty street and reached into his blazer pocket. His fingers rummaged beneath the 38 Special, and he pulled out his little glass vial for one more hit.

SIXTEEN

'm ready for things to go back to normal," Maggie said as she looked away from the patio and back at Wyatt. He frowned at her, and she suddenly felt self-conscious. "I mean, life in general."

"That would be a pleasant turn of events," he said.

Around the time Maggie became uncomfortable with his scrutiny, Wyatt seemed to want to change the subject and pretend things already were normal. He rapped his knuckles on the counter.

"Are you hungry?" Wyatt asked Maggie.

She shook her head. "No. Thanks. We ate."

He opened up the fridge. "Well, I'm feeling peckish. How about a snack?"

"Go ahead and eat," she said, watching him poke at a couple of the take-out containers stacked in his fridge.

He smelled a Styrofoam box, winced, and put it back in the fridge. "I ate," he said, closing the fridge. "The cool thing about having cereal for dinner is that you don't have to bother with breakfast the next day."

He turned around and opened one of the cupboards.

"You really need to eat more like a grown-up," Maggie said.

He threw her a look. "Says the woman whose lunch I usually have to finish," he said. "Oh look, Cheetos." He grabbed the half-full bag out of the cupboard and closed the door.

"That's so sad, Wyatt," Maggie said.

He slapped the bag onto the breakfast bar. "Well, I can put them on a salad if it makes you feel better."

"You don't have anything for a salad," she said, rubbing at her right eye, in which her contact was threatening to fold up.

"Well, then I can put some ranch dressing on them."

Maggie felt a smile forming. "You're so cute when you're idiotic."

"Is that why you're winking at me?"

"I don't know how to wink," she said. "It's my contacts."

Wyatt finished chewing his Cheeto. "You wear contacts?"

"Yeah," she said, as though he were a moron. "How can you not know that?"

"Huh. Are your eyes really green?"

"Yes," she said, shaking her head.

She slid down from the stool and bent down to reach into her purse. She pulled out her saline and her contact case.

"You want some more wine?"

Maggie stood back up. "Yeah, sure. I'll be right back," she said.

She walked around the corner and down the hall to the bathroom, set her contact case on the sink.

"You wanna go out on the patio?" Wyatt called out to her.

"Yeah," she called back, and unscrewed the cap of her contact case, then leaned in to look in the mirror as she pulled up her eyelid.

⚓   ⚓   ⚓

Wyatt ate another Cheeto, then he poured Maggie another glass of wine, topped off his own, and put the wine back in the fridge.

He picked up the two glasses and walked into the dining area. Patrick was standing just inside the French doors, his arm stretched out toward Wyatt. Wyatt had just enough time to think about diving for the kitchen floor. He even managed to start to pivot to the right before Patrick fired, and pain and heat exploded in Wyatt's lower abdomen.

He heard the sound of the wine glasses shattering, saw the bottom of the refrigerator as his face hit the cold tile floor. Then there was just nothing.

⚓   ⚓   ⚓

Maggie dropped the contact lens in the sink as the gunshot rang out.

She froze, stopped breathing, and listened, but heard nothing. The only thing she could see through the open bathroom door was the edge of Wyatt's bedroom door across the dark hall.

She pressed her lips shut before she could call out to Wyatt. If he hadn't called out to her first, it was either because he couldn't or because he shouldn't. She reached around to the back of her jeans and her entire body went cold. She wasn't wearing her holster. Her service weapon was in her purse. Out there.

She very carefully took one step closer to the bathroom door, gently setting the rubber sole of her hiking boot down on the tile. Then she took two slow, silent breaths, breathing out through her mouth, consciously trying to slow her heart and quiet the pounding of blood in her ears.

Then she leaned forward and listened.

⚓ ⚓ ⚓

Patrick stepped slowly toward the kitchen area, stopped before he got to the half wall that blocked his view of the kitchen itself. He hadn't expected Wyatt to come around the corner, but he had. After, he'd expected Maggie to come flying out from the kitchen, but she hadn't.

He waited by the wall and listened. The only things he could hear were the sounds of the rain pattering behind him and the hum of the refrigerator. He didn't hear a sound from Wyatt, but he'd seen the red spot blossoming on his stomach before he'd even dived for the floor. He knew he'd hit him. He just wasn't sure how good, or whether Wyatt had a gun in there.

He listened for a few more seconds, then took another cautious step forward and leaned out enough to see part of the kitchen. Wyatt's feet, barefoot soles up. He watched the feet for a few more seconds, then stepped around.

Glass crunched underneath his feet, and he froze. Wyatt was partly on his right side, partly on his stomach, his head up against the fridge. His eyes were closed, his hands still and empty. Patrick watched his face, but it didn't even twitch. There was no flickering around the eyelids.

Patrick blinked as a rain drop slid from his hair to his own eyelid. Then he took another step forward, his eyes darting back and forth between Wyatt and the living room. He could see almost the entire room and he was pretty sure she wasn't in it.

The only door was the front door. That had to be a hall-way wall on the other side of the breakfast bar. She would be there. Maybe right there. He raised his arm, trained the gun in that general direction while he looked back down at Wyatt. There was no blood on his back, though there was already a pool of it beginning underneath him.

Patrick glanced once more at the wall, then shoved at Wyatt's hip with his foot. Wyatt rolled over onto his back after the second push. Man, he was a mess. He thought maybe Wyatt's chest was moving, but he couldn't be sure. He wasn't going to lean over and check, and he wasn't walking around that corner so she could blow his ass away, either.

He needed his own corner, his own wall. She could come to him, but he still had an appointment with the old man. He'd go out, but he'd go out when he was done.

⚓ ⚓ ⚓

Maggie heard the sound of broken glass on tile, the sound of someone stepping slowly on broken glass. Wyatt was in his bare feet. Whoever was there was in the kitchen or dining area, she knew that. She swallowed as she won-dered where Wyatt was, then made herself shift her focus. Could be one person, could be more. But it *felt* like one. She could feel the occupancy the way a person could walk into a house and feel that they were the only one there.

She heard another soft crunching of glass, and she took a quiet breath and poked her head just far enough around the doorway to see the hall. There was no one in it, but she hadn't expected there to be.

She could see nothing of the kitchen area, except the line where the tile began, right at the wall of the kitchen. Her head felt naked, exposed, and the hairs on it responded by standing up, her scalp jerking like a spider had just walked up her leg.

She pulled her head back in and lowered herself to a crouch, listened. Nothing. She needed to get across the hallway, to see if she could see into the dining area. She had no way to tell if the person stepped on the glass on their way in or on their way out. Whoever it was might not even know there was someone else in the house.

She remembered her purse sitting on the floor by the breakfast bar and her stomach turned over.

Being out in the hallway when someone turned that corner would be fatal. But waiting in the bathroom wasn't going to be any less so. And Wyatt was out there.

She slowly eased her head back through the doorway.

"Really, Maggie? You and Wyatt?" a man's voice called.

She jerked her head back in, her heart pounding even harder than it had been. Who was that? She knew she recognized the voice. Her brain started whipping through a mental Rolodex of men's voices.

"What a stereotype," the man called out. Maggie's eyes focused on the toilet paper holder across from her as she sorted through voices in her head.

"Hey, Maggie, does my father know?" the man called, and then laughed, almost a giggle.

Maggie's mouth opened and then closed. Patrick? Her eyes darted around as she tried to process that as quickly as possible. What the hell? Her first, useless thought was that he was pissed about the search at Sea-Fair, and she immediately brushed over it. She knew Patrick's opinion of Wyatt was mostly disdain, and that he couldn't stand her. But that wasn't something for a very public man to throw everything away for. He was the Assistant State's Attorney. He was rich. He was a Boudreaux.

A Boudreaux. *I'm tired of cleaning up Boudreaux's messes.* She felt a quick swell of nausea as she realized that she hadn't just withheld information in a case, she had become incapable of working one. If Harper had said Smith, she wouldn't have just picked one Smith out of the phone book and decided it was him. Why had she been so stupid?

A small voice reminded her that she had just watched David get killed, and that she had just been shot. That her entire month had been surreal and mind-bending. She quelled the voice quickly; she didn't have time to excuse herself. She needed to get out there and find Wyatt. She needed to get out there and get her gun.

She took a shallow breath and eased her head back out the doorway. She heard a scraping noise she couldn't define. She still couldn't tell exactly where he was. Which side of the breakfast bar he was on was the difference between suicide and possible survival.

She got up on the balls of her feet, then silently dashed slightly diagonally across the hall to Wyatt's bedroom, being careful not to brush against the open door. She took a second to catch her breath and listen, as she crouched just inside the room.

"Your *other* boyfriend's not looking too good, Maggie," Patrick called. Then he spoke at a more normal volume. "You slut."

Maggie pushed the fear and then the anger down, shoved them into their own box and closed the lid. Then she blinked a few times. The vision in her right eye was blurry, but she could think around it. She just needed to stay cool. She edged closer to the doorway and peeked.

Wyatt's room was only about a foot closer to the living area, and it didn't provide her a much better view. But when she leaned out just a bit further, she could see part of the wall across from the kitchen, and there she saw Patrick's shadow. She was pretty sure he was in the actual kitchen.

She heard him step on more glass as she pulled herself back into Wyatt's room. He wasn't bothering to be stealthy anymore. She heard something move on the counter.

"You know, you should be grateful, Maggie," Patrick said, his voice just slightly louder than a conversational volume. "If Pop found out you were sleeping around on him, he'd kill you. And I promise you he wouldn't do it nearly so nicely."

Maggie took a couple of breaths and closed her eyes for just a second, saw the hallway in her mind, measured her distance. She was dead if he walked around that bar and looked. But she was dead either way.

She looked back out the doorway, saw the shadow moving, and waited. It stopped, and she heard him move or put something hard on the counter.

She blinked once, slowly, and in the space of time that her eyes were closed, she saw Kyle swing at a curve ball, felt Sky's head on her back at the sink. Then she pushed herself out into the hall.

Once there, she stood up slowly, and put her back to the wall but not on it. It wouldn't matter which side of the hall she was on if he took a look around the corner, but she needed to try to keep an eye on his shadow.

"Hey Maggie? It occurs to me that I'm basically cleaning up your entire love life for you," Patrick said. "First your hubby, now Wyatt, and pretty soon your sugar daddy. I bet that rankles, huh?"

Maggie slowed her breathing to almost nothing and made herself stare at a scratch on the opposite wall, until she could zone out everything that he had just said. She waited a moment, until she felt the cold, slow, wave of calm flow into her mind, then started inching her way down the hall, her eyes on the dining area wall. He was moving, but standing in one place.

"I don't have all night, Maggie," he called. "Gotta go see the old man."

Maggie kept moving, and when she was about three feet from the end of the hall, she switched sides. She heard a sound she couldn't quite make out. It didn't make sense to her. She stopped, her back nearly against the wall, six inches of drywall separating her from Patrick. She listened, and blinked when she heard the noise again. He was eating the damn Cheetos.

She slowly sank down into a crouch, and crabbed her way another foot or so toward the kitchen. She heard him doing something else at the counter and stopped.

"Aw. I broke my little spoon," she heard him say to himself.

She edged forward again, and came to the end of the wall. She got on her knees so she could lean forward just a bit, then tilted her head toward the breakfast bar. Her purse was there, under the closest stool, but it was still about three feet away, too far to just reach out and grab it.

She started inching forward on her hands and knees. Patrick, sounding so close, sniffed and then coughed softly. She laid down on her stomach, praying he wasn't tall enough to see her, and reached out for her bag.

She tried to mentally inventory her purse, to remember what would jingle, what would clink, as she slid it slowly onto the carpet, then pulled it back with her. She got back up into a crouch at the end of the wall, then reached into her purse and put her hands on her holster. She slid the Glock 23 from her purse, and only remembered to breathe once she had it against her chest.

She needed to make a decision. There was no way she'd be able to pull back the slide without him hearing it, and if he heard it, he wasn't stupid enough to walk around the corner and let her blow him away. He would wait, and he would be far more ready than he already was. He could wait indefinitely, but Wyatt was in there somewhere, and she could not.

She got as low as she could on her hands and knees, sliding the Glock along on the carpet. When she could go no further that way without the gun hitting tile, she eased herself into the lowest squat she'd ever managed, the gun in both hands on her chest, listening as she heard the rustling of cloth.

Then she didn't need to make any more decisions. In the space of a heartbeat, she heard Wyatt groan, heard Patrick cry out, then heard the hammer of a revolver.

She pulled the slide as she jumped up, and was already aiming when she cleared the breakfast bar. Patrick was in the middle of swinging his gun toward the floor.

She shot him three times. The first one went into the middle of his back, and as his body jerked around from the impact, she shot him twice more in the chest. He looked up at her between the second and third shots, and he looked more irritated than surprised.

SEVENTEEN

Maggie stood on the foot rail of the stool, trying to see what was happening on the floor, but even if she had been tall enough, she wouldn't have been able to see Wyatt past the backs of the two EMTs.

There were too many people in Wyatt's small kitchen. In addition to Wyatt, Patrick and the two EMTs, Terry Coyle was taking pictures of the scene, as one of Larry Davenport's assistants examined Patrick's body.

A handful of deputies and PD walked in and out of the house, and she understood another handful were outside, keeping the street clear for the EMTs and keeping the neighbors at bay.

Maggie had given a brief initial statement to Terry and handed over her weapon, but he had left her pretty much alone for the duration. Maggie checked her old Timex and saw that it had only been twelve minutes since she'd called 911, and only nine since the EMTs and the first Apalach PD car had arrived. Dwight, and then Terry, had been one or two minutes behind.

To Maggie, the nine minutes had seemed like an hour. She had been yelled at twice already for asking why they weren't just going to the hospital, had been told sharply by Carl Rosen, one of the EMTs, that Wyatt needed to be stabilized.

She had stopped asking when she heard the other EMT bark something about Wyatt's blood pressure dropping, then heard them use the paddles on Wyatt. She had felt the current in her own chest.

"Okay, let's go," she heard Carl say quickly. "James, give us a hand?"

The assistant medical examiner stood, and the three men lifted the board on which Wyatt was lying and grunted as they placed him onto the gurney that waited at the end of the breakfast bar. Maggie got a quick look at Wyatt's pale face before Carl got in the way.

"I'm going with you," Maggie said.

"No, you're following, Maggie," Carl said as he unlocked the wheels with his foot. "No room."

They rushed past her, and she saw Dwight coming back inside. She snatched up her purse as he walked up to her.

"Is there anybody behind my Jeep?" she asked, rushing past him and making him pivot mid-stride.

"Uh, I don't know."

"I need to get out," she said.

"Hey, uh, we called Boudreaux. He's out there."

"I don't care," Maggie said as she rushed out the screen door.

"I'm just saying," he said as he followed.

Maggie wasn't sure how many vehicles were outside. Red and blue lights swiped across her black Cherokee from every direction, but there was one PD car parked behind her in the driveway.

"I need to get out!" she shouted to the yard in general, as she hurried down the walkway. One of the Apalach uniforms looked over at her and rushed to the driver's side of the patrol car that was blocking her.

Maggie looked at the street in front of Wyatt's house. Little pockets of people lined the sidewalk across the street, some of them in uniform. A little old lady in a purple bathrobe looked at Maggie in horror, and Maggie looked down. Her hands were smeared with Wyatt's blood, and her shirt was covered with it. She had a flash of the night, just a few weeks ago, when she had looked down and seen that David's blood had drenched her tee shirt. The déjà vu almost made her vomit, and she pushed the memory away.

The EMTs roared off toward Weems Memorial, and as they did, she saw Boudreaux across the street. He was facing her, hands on his hips and looking down at the sidewalk, as a uniform spoke to him.

He looked up as Maggie reached her Jeep. He looked right at her, and their eyes met for just a moment before she jumped into the Jeep.

She waited for the cruiser to back into the street, then she pulled out. As she stopped and put the Jeep in drive, she looked out her window. Boudreaux was right there on the sidewalk, just five or six feet away. The tears on his cheeks looked almost yellow in the light from the streetlamp behind him.

Maggie hit the gas and pulled away.

Two days later, Maggie sat in the recliner next to Wyatt's hospital bed, as she had the night he'd come in, as she had the day before. She had left the hospital only to go to her parents, hug the kids, shower, swallow something, and return. Her Dad had been running to the house to feed the chickens, and Coco was content in her parents' back yard.

She was, for the second time in less than two months, on administrative leave until the investigation of the shooting was completed. There was nowhere else she needed to be.

The night he'd been brought in, Wyatt had been in surgery for more than five hours. The bullet had done a great deal of damage to his left hip, as well as his small intestine. He had lost a lot of blood.

As Maggie understood it, an orthopedic surgeon had worked on the hip once the small intestine had been virtually removed, spliced, and put back in place. Wyatt's doctor had explained to her that it was essential for Wyatt's hip to be completely immobile, so they were keeping him under anesthesia for a few days. They'd put him into a medically induced coma.

Despite the fact that they assured her they would call and let her know when they were bringing him out of it, Maggie preferred to wait. It wasn't until the second day that Maggie had learned that Wyatt, when he'd been treated in the ER last year for a concussion, had listed her as his next of kin.

She'd sat there staring at his still hand for more than five minutes, wondering how this beautiful man had come to be so alone that she was his next of kin.

She'd wondered a lot of things during the hours that she had sat next to Wyatt's bed.

She knew that she had lost her ability to work effectively, to think effectively, as a cop. She had, for a time, confided more in a known criminal, one whose motives were a mystery, than she had in the man who had become more than her closest friend.

From the moment she had walked onto the beach on the island, and looked down at what was left of Gregory Boudreaux's shattered face, she had been changing, drifting away from who and what she was. She felt like the frog in the pot of slowly boiling water. It had been so gradual, so imperceptible, that she had let it happen, had given her consent by virtue of the fact that she hadn't run.

Maggie sighed and leaned back in the recliner, trying to find some position that she hadn't already worn out. She couldn't, so she stood up and stretched her back, looked at her watch. It was almost four in the afternoon, and she would need to leave soon.

She heard the door swish open behind her, and looked to see Dwight coming in, wearing jeans and a button down shirt.

"Hey, Maggie," he said quietly.

"Hey."

"How's he doing?"

"He's the same. His vitals are good. They scanned his hip earlier, and they said it's looking good."

Dwight put a hand on the bed rail and looked at Wyatt. "He's gonna be pissed about that nightie they got on him."

Maggie smiled. "Yeah."

"Uh, so, Tomlinson's looking for you," he said.

"I'm on leave," she said.

"Yeah, I know, but he wanted to talk to you. He said to call him and he'd meet you."

Maggie looked over at Wyatt. "All right."

"The service is tomorrow night," Dwight said. "You comin'?"

"Yeah."

John Solomon, her former colleague turned Chamber of Commerce exec, had rallied local business owners, churches and civic groups, and in a matter of two days enough money or other donations had been collected to give the Guatemalans a proper burial, albeit a very basic one.

The florists, William and Robert, had donated simple posies to be tossed into the sea from the beach. A local hardware store had donated most of their stock of emergency candles. The donation money had gone toward the actual burials. Since there weren't enough spaces in one section of the cemetery, a graveside service was impossible, so they were doing a memorial on the beach instead.

Maggie looked at Dwight. "I was getting ready to leave, anyway," she said.

"When are they waking him up?"

"Tomorrow some time. But they won't let anyone be here," she said. "They said it's better if he doesn't have company."

"Oh. Well, I figured I'd hang out a little while today," Dwight said.

Maggie smiled. "That's cool, Dwight. Thanks."

"You should try to take it easy maybe tomorrow. Not to hurt your feelings, but you don't look so hot."

"Awesome, thanks," she said.

She picked up her purse and turned to leave.

"Hey, Maggie?" She turned around, and Dwight licked his lips nervously before he spoke. "It's good, you and Wyatt. You know?"

Maggie blinked at him a couple of times. "He's my boss. And my friend."

"Look, I'm a simple guy, but I'm not stupid," he said gently. "It's good, you and Wyatt," he repeated.

Maggie tried to find some other words to say that they were just friends, something that wasn't a lie and wasn't a straight out confession that it had started to be good, but was probably done. She couldn't come up with anything, so she just nodded and walked out of the room.

⚓ ⚓ ⚓

Maggie met Tomlinson on the patio at Caroline's, a restaurant overlooking the river just a block from his hotel.

He waited until he'd been served his coffee and she had her sweet tea, then he leaned on the table and folded his hands.

"So, we're sending the boy home day after tomorrow," he said without preamble.

Maggie's stomach turned over. "Sending him back? They won't let him stay? He's just a kid."

"He doesn't want to stay, Lieutenant. He wants to go home to his grandparents."

Maggie sat back, feeling deflated and maybe even just a little bit rejected.

"But you said it's terrible where his people are," she said weakly.

"It's not great," he admitted. "But the kid just lost his parents and his only sibling. He doesn't care that it's not great. He doesn't give a crap about what the US has to offer him at this point. He just wants to go home to people that know him."

"Is he coming to the memorial service?"

"No. But he does want to stop by his family's graves before he leaves."

Maggie sighed and looked out toward the river, then back at Tomlinson. "Is he flying out of Panama City?"

"No, we've got a plane taking us to Tallahassee, then I'm handing him off to another agent who'll escort him to Dallas and then on to Guatemala."

Maggie stared at her tea a moment.

"Would you like to drive him to Regional?" Tomlinson shrugged a little as Maggie looked at him. "I could just meet you there."

"Yes." She swallowed something that felt like it might become tears. "Thank you."

EIGHTEEN

Maggie passed the next day in a flurry of activity. She needed normalcy more than she needed rest, and she needed to keep busy. She, the kids, and Coco had come home, endured extensive scolding from Stoopid, and tried to settle back into their lives.

Maggie cleaned, did laundry, helped Kyle clean out the chicken coop, and yanked all of the bygone vegetables from the raised bed garden. In between, she wondered if Wyatt was awake, and what he was thinking if he was. She wondered what she would say to a little boy who didn't know or care about her. She wondered whether she should ever return from leave.

An hour or so before sunset, she and the kids headed out to St. George Island. When they got to the empty lots next to Boudreaux's rental, they weren't empty anymore. Cars were parked all along the driveways that had no houses, and they lined the street as well. Maggie parked on the side of the road, and they walked over the dunes to the beach.

Maggie was surprised, and moved, by the number of people who were there. Many were locals, but some appeared to be tourists. She and the kids were handed candles by women from the Junior League, who had set up a card table, then they found Maggie's parents down the beach.

Just after eight o'clock, William and Robert walked down the line of people standing near the shoreline, and handed small bunches of flowers to each.

At 8:37, as the sun began to set over the water, someone up the beach began to play "Amazing Grace" on the flute, and a thousand little flowers were cast into the sea.

⚓   ⚓   ⚓

At just after nine the next morning, Wyatt's doctor called and let Maggie know that she could visit him. He assured her that Wyatt was doing well, but he couldn't have answered any of the other questions Maggie had.

When she walked into the hospital room, her heart was pounding uncomfortably in her chest, and she knew her hands were shaking. She swallowed, and walked around the room divider next to Wyatt's bed.

He was lying there looking out the second floor window at nothing much. Maggie was relieved to see that he looked a lot more like himself without the intubation tube, but he still looked pale.

He looked over at her as she rounded the divider, and she tried to smile as she stopped and put a hand on the bed rail.

"Hey," she said.

"Hey." His voice sounded like he'd been in the desert for a month, and he cleared his throat just a little.

"How are you feeling?" she asked, thinking it was a stupid thing to say.

"Okay." He looked out the window again. "I was just lying here thinking." He looked back at her. "You know how, on TV, cops get shot and they grimace like somebody punched them in the arm, then they say something really witty and kill the bad guys?"

Maggie's upper lip curled up in part of a smile. "Yeah?"

"That's a lot of crap," he croaked. "It hurts like hell. I was conscious there for a little bit, I think I remember the EMTs being there, and I couldn't come up with a single quip."

Maggie blew out a breath. "Yeah."

"Oh, yeah, you would know. I forgot."

They looked at each other a moment, and Maggie took a deep breath.

"Wyatt, I have to leave in just a few minutes, to take Virgilio to the airport, but I need to tell you some things."

"They're deporting the kid?" he asked, frowning.

"No. He wants to go home to his family," Maggie said. Wyatt nodded, and she went on. "I've been thinking. A lot. About the last couple of months, and about the other night."

"Okay," he said.

"I don't think I should come back from leave," she said.

"Why?"

Maggie looked down at her fingers in the rail. "Everything. Everything that I have screwed up lately. The reasons I screwed them up." She looked up at Wyatt. She couldn't read his face, and it scared her. "But yesterday, I was sitting here, and I was thinking about the other night. And about Ricky Alessi."

"Ricky Alessi was about to blow your head off, Maggie."

"Yeah, I know. And to save my own life, I put a bullet in his chest."

"Which is what you needed to do. Nobody's ever questioned that. We were all there."

"I know. But I shot him one time. I put three rounds into Patrick Boudreaux. Three." Maggie took a breath and let it out slowly. "I was scared, for you, and for me. But more than being scared, I was enraged. I was covered in it, filled with it. I put three rounds into that bastard when I only needed one. I can't help but wonder if, subconsciously, it was one for David, one for you, and one for me."

"Maggie, you didn't do anything outside the lines the other night."

"*I'm* outside the lines, Wyatt." She sighed, and looked down at his wrist band for a moment to gather her thoughts. "There's something else, though."

"What?"

"I need you to just listen and then I'm going to go, okay? I don't really want you to respond."

"Can I say okay right now?"

Maggie sighed. "Wyatt." She looked him in the eye. "I know there's distance between us right now. I know I've done some things, and we've—we're not where we were a week ago. And what you said about David and I—"

"I was out of line."

"No. No, you really weren't that far off. The truth is, I don't remember ever actually being in the act of falling in love with David. I just loved him. But I always had."

She swallowed and made herself hold his gaze. "I never got nervous around him or stayed awake thinking about him or felt like I was turning inside out when he looked at me."

She chewed her lip and had to look down at his chin for a moment, because it was so much easier than looking him in the eye. "The thing is, if at some point you decide that I'm not too damaged, or that this isn't completely wrecked, I'd like to be able to just be with you. I don't want to worry about our jobs or being caught or being sneaky."

She cleared her throat and hiked her purse up onto her shoulder.

"Are you leaving?" he asked her.

She couldn't look him in the face. "I need to go get Virgilio."

She stalked out of the room before he could say anything, and was standing at the elevator when her cell vibrated in her pocket. She pulled it out, didn't recognize the number.

"Hello?"

"It wouldn't kill either one of us if you were to run downstairs to the vending machine and get me a Mountain Dew," Wyatt said.

"What?"

"I asked Nurse Ratchet to bring me one, but she wouldn't," he said. "I tried the eyebrow wiggle and everything. She might be a lesbian."

Three minutes later, Maggie walked back into Wyatt's room with a bottle of Mountain Dew. She unscrewed the cap and held it out to him.

"Can you just set it down?"

Maggie put it on the tray table next to his bed, and Wyatt reached up and grabbed her other hand, tugged her down to him, and kissed her gently on the mouth.

"Bring me a grown-up size when you come back from the airport," he said, and reached for his remote.

Maggie stood at the rope gate in the terminal, and watched as Tomlinson stopped to speak to the flight attendant for the commuter jet.

Virgilio stood patiently beside him, Kyle's backpack at his feet. He was looking away from Maggie, watching another plane taxi to a stop outside the window.

Maggie hadn't said much to him on the way there. She couldn't think of anything that wasn't a platitude or a way to just make herself feel better. So she stuck to talking to him about flying in a plane for the first time, and pretended she was saying something meaningful. She hoped that he knew that she wished she could.

Tomlinson turned around and raised a hand at Maggie as he picked up the backpack, and she raised one back. Virgilio glanced over his shoulder at her, then he followed Tomlinson to the gangway, Mickey Mouse in hand, looking like a little boy who had just been on a visit to Disney World, and was now going home to tell his friends.

She watched him disappear from sight, then turned and walked away.

⚓ ⚓ ⚓

THE END

Read on for a sneak peek at
Landfall, the fourth book in the
Forgotten Coast Suspense series.

www.dawnleemckenna.com

GET UNFORGOTTEN

To get UnForgotten, and be the first to hear about new releases, special pricing for friends of the series and fun news about the books and Apalach, please subscribe to the newsletter.

I'd like to extend a special thank you to so many of you who pre-ordered your copy of *What Washes Up*.

You let me know after reading *Low Tide* that you wanted to keep reading this series almost as much as I want to keep writing it. I was overwhelmed by the number of pre-orders, and it meant a great deal to me that you wanted to spend more time with these characters. It's because of you that I knew that Maggie, Wyatt and Boudreaux had an audience.

As always, your honest review would be deeply appreciated. If you could take a moment to share your experience with *What Washes Up,* I would be thrilled.

Also, feel free to drop me a line anytime, at

dawnmckenna63@gmail.com

I love hearing from readers.

LANDFALL

August 12th
3:36pm
Hurricane Nora 27.0N 83.4W

Maggie laid on the table for two pounding heart-beats, then slid off and onto her feet, and scrambled over to Sky's chair.

"Mom, what just happened?" Sky asked, her voice near hysterical.

"I don't know," Maggie said, squatting behind Sky's chair and furiously working the ropes that bound her wrists.

"What did he do?"

"I don't know, Sky!"

The wind was whistling like a train outside, and it seemed impossible that it could be louder than it had already been. Maggie looked up toward the kitchen window as something small but hard hit it, and she caught Kyle's eye. He was staring at the front door, his eyes wide.

"I'm coming, Kyle," Maggie said. He looked at her, but didn't say anything.

Sky wiggled her fingers. "Hurry, Mom!"

"Hold still, baby, please," Maggie said.

She yanked the ropes free and jumped up as Sky pulled her arms around to the front. They were stiff from hours of being bound behind her, and she rolled them gingerly.

"Sky, I need you to grab the Glock," Maggie said, as she squatted behind Kyle and started working on the ropes. His thin wrists were bleeding, and the ropes had left welts on them that made Maggie want to scream.

Sky ran over to the kitchen counter and picked up the Glock, where it lay with the Mossberg and her great-grand-father's .38. "Do you want me to bring it to you?"

"No, I need it for you," she said. "Do you remember how to use it?"

"Yeah, but...I guess. Why not the .38?"

"This is not the time for a revolver, baby," Maggie answered. "Just take it. I want you take it, and I want you to take Kyle, and I want you guys to go in your room, and you don't come out unless I come get you."

"Mom, wait—"

"You don't come out unless I come get you, do you understand me?" Maggie yelled.

"Yes."

A branch slammed into the window behind Sky, and she ducked instinctively, but the glass didn't break. The branch fell away again as she straightened up and grabbed the extra rounds from the counter and shoved them into her pocket.

Maggie finally pulled Kyle's wrists free, and she rubbed them for just a second before she pulled him up from the chair. "Kyle, you go with Sky, and you guys stay in there. Do you hear me?"

"Yeah," he said, his voice a croak.

"Go!" Maggie barked at Sky, and the kids ran down the hallway. As soon as she heard their steps, Coco started barking and scratching at the door again. Maggie watched Sky open the door, watched the kids go in and slam the door behind them, then she ran over to the kitchen counter.

She glanced up at the front door several times, as she loaded the Mossberg, shoved a couple of extra rounds in her shorts pocket, and then ran over to the door. The floor was wet from when he had burst through, and she slipped and nearly went down before catching herself.

She put an ear to the door, but it was a ridiculous thing to do. On the other side was nothing but noise, and she could hear nothing beyond the pounding of the rain on the deck.

She took a deep breath, slammed back the action on the shotgun, and flung open the door.

Boudreaux was in the yard, a few feet from the bottom of the stairs. He was almost knee deep in water from the river, and the water closest to him was colored a deep, dark red.

He looked up at her, the wind buffeting him and pushing him, his hair whipping wildly.

Maggie raised the shotgun and felt a catch in her throat as she looked into those eyes, so deeply blue even from this distance.

"I wish you hadn't come here, Mr. Boudreaux."

⚓　⚓　⚓

Coming August 2015

9 780692 501689